PRAISE FOR THE FIERY TALES

"Wickedly passionate . . . [A] sensual treat!"
—**Sylvia Day,**
#1 *New York Times* bestselling author

"Hot enough to warm the coldest winter night."
—**Publishers Weekly**

"Lushly erotic . . . Sophisticated and deeply romantic."
—**Elizabeth Hoyt,**
New York Times bestselling author

"Sure to delight!"
—**Jennifer Ashley,**
New York Times bestselling author

"The most luscious, sexy take on classic fairy tales I've ever read!"
—**Cheryl Holt,**
New York Times bestselling author

LILA DIPASQUA

Excerpt from *Little Red Writing*, by Lila DiPasqua copyright © Lila DiPasqua
Cover design by Seductive Designs
Photography by Period Images
Interior Design by Woven Red Author Services, www.WovenRed.ca

PRINTING HISTORY
First Edition: From *Awakened by a Kiss*, Berkley Sensation/Penguin Group (USA) Inc.—August 2010
Second Edition: Lila DiPasqua—December 2015

ISBN: 978-0-9880350-7-2 (trade pbk)
ISBN: 978-0-9880350-6-5 (e-book)

To my angels above.
Thank you.

A HISTORICAL TIDBIT

The hero in this story, Adrien Christophe d'Aspe de Bourbon, Marquis de Beaulain, was not entirely born of this author's imagination.

In actual fact, Adrien was inspired by the Baron de Chantal. Who on earth was the Baron de Chantal, you ask?

Well, if you were a woman in seventeenth century France, you'd be very much aware of the Baron de Chantal. Tall, and sinfully gorgeous. A master swordsman, expert horseman, dancer, charmer extraordinaire and ladies' man. And though dueling was against the law, he'd fought more than his share. But Adrien wasn't inspired by just a handsome, charming, historical bad boy. It was what happened to Chantal when he was young that made him stand out to me.

And shaped Adrien's character.

You see, Chantal's mother, the Baroness Jeanne de Chantal, a widow, abandoned him and his two sisters to enter the convent and take the veil (later to become canonized by the Catholic Church and made Saint Jeanne de Chantal in 1767). On the day his mother was to leave, the young, future Baron de Chantal at the time, flung himself across the doorway of their home in tears over her departure. Ignoring his pleas, she stepped over him, and left him to be raised by his uncle. As a mother, I was heartsick for him. And that very painful, life-altering event no doubt changed who he was inside—as well as my hero Adrien, who had the very same anguished-filled event occur in his life.

As to what happened to the Baron de Chantal, he eventually married and his daughter was the famous, Marquise de Sévigné—best known for her letters to her daughter that spanned thirty years, and have been published as a collection in different languages around the world. Like her father, Marquise de Sévigné was incredibly bright and charming and welcomed into all the prestigious salons in Paris where the aristocracy and literati gathered to discuss and debate things like politics, philosophy, grammar and books. She is recognized as someone who was influential in shaping the French language, and literature.

It was during this same time period that French writer Charles Perrault, creator of *The Tales of Mother Goose,* (and the genre of fairy tales) attended the same salons and went on to write stories that have delighted people for centuries: *Sleeping Beauty, Little Red Riding Hood, Puss in Boots, Bluebeard,* and the ever-popular *Cinderella,* to name a few.

The following is loosely based on *Sleeping Beauty*—and the Baron de Chantal. Step into the glittering and salacious world when fairy tales were born…

Happy Reading!

SLEEPING BEAU

Moral of the Story of Sleeping Beauty:

To wait so long,
To want a man refined and strong,
Is not at all uncommon.
But: rare it is a hundred years to wait.
Indeed there is no woman
Today so patient for a mate.
Our tale was meant to show
That when marriage is deferred,
It is no less blissful than those of which you've heard.
Nothing's lost after a century or so.
And yet, for lovers whose ardor
Cannot be controlled and marry out of passion,
I don't have the heart their act to deplore
Or to preach a moral lesson.

Charles Perrault (1628–1703)

CHAPTER ONE

France, 1685

"Will you do it, Adrien? Say yes. You simply must. I'm your *sister*." Charlotte's whine taxed Adrien's already thin patience.

Adrien Christophe d'Aspe de Bourbon, Marquis de Beaulain, stared out the window at the gardens below. Lords and ladies milled about, clustering near the fountains and along the pathways bordered by flowerbeds. His mood was foul. His audience with his father the root cause. It hadn't gone well. It never went well. Days after the fact, he was still irritable. He'd only just arrived at the Comtesse de Lamotte's château and already Charlotte had him wanting to leave. Her unexpected presence and the absurd scheme she'd devised had effectively soured his plans: a few days at Suzanne's abode, indulging in drink and debauchery to lift him out of his ill humor.

"You are my half-sister, Charlotte. We have *different* fathers," he replied bitterly. Raised in Paris at the Hôtel d'Aspe by his three uncles, Adrien had had all the male influence he'd needed. Or wanted. Except for the occasional horrid visit, his father had been absent from his life—that is, until a year ago when Adrien's mother had died. Since then Louis had injected himself into Adrien's world. Though Adrien wanted nothing to do with the man, his father was not someone he or anyone could simply ignore.

Charlotte rose from the settee and stopped beside him. "You needn't remind me of that. Your father is the King. At least he has legitimized you, given you title and lands—"

"He legitimized all his illegitimate children. Not just me. And it is a wonder there's any land left in the realm, given the multitude he sired. I doubt even he knows how many mistresses he's had." Their mother among the masses.

"Well, the Baron de Chambly still won't recognize me as his. He's never given me a moment's thought, much less wealth."

"Charlotte, *nothing* comes without a price." His tone dripped with disdain.

"Come now, Adrien. Enough of this. We are family. *I need you.*" Her bottom lip was out in a full pout. "What I ask of you is not so strenuous. You and I both know you'll bed a woman or two here before the week is up. All I ask is that you bed Catherine de Villecourt as well. Charm her. Convince her that marriage is not what she wants. Lure her away from my Philbert. You're my only hope, Adrien. He's set to wed her in two weeks." Tears glistened in her hazel eyes. "I don't want to lose him. He's been so distant lately. I fear if he weds, I'll never get him back. She's younger than I. Fifteen years his junior." Two tears spilled down her cheeks. "He'll focus on his new bride and forget all about me."

Exasperated, Adrien let out a sharp breath. Charlotte and their mother were so alike. She, too, had harbored the illusion that she could accomplish the impossible: maintain her lover's interest indefinitely and remain his favorite for good.

"Charlotte, find yourself a new lover. You don't need Philbert de Baillet."

"Yes I do," she protested. "I love him! I don't want to live without him."

How many times had he heard those very words from his mother's mouth about his father? Love. It was highly overrated. He'd no idea why anyone would pursue it. Love caused suffering. Lust was much easier to deal with. And far more pleasurable.

Adrien was about to rebut when she added, "Look down there. There she is now. With our hostess."

Mildly curious about Charlotte's rival, he glanced down at the manicured grounds and spotted their hostess Suzanne de Lamotte. She was with a woman whose rich auburn hair looked a tad too familiar. He stared harder. From this distance, he couldn't make out enough details to be certain . . . but . . . The hair on the back of his neck stood on end. *Dieu*, it looked like *her*.

Could it possibly be . . . ?

Visions of the redhead naked in his bed materialized in his mind. He still remembered her face. Her scent—jasmine. And the sultry sounds she made each time she came. Their carnal encounter was like none he'd ever known. Perfect spine-melting passion. Her delectable mouth, her lush form, and her hot silky sex clasped snugly around his thrusting cock had him on fire the entire night.

In the morning, he was shocked to discover that she'd spiked his burgundy with an aphrodisiac. And she was gone. He'd been confused, a bit disoriented, and uncertain if the whole thing hadn't been a dream. But the scent of jasmine lingered on his skin.

And on the sheets, glaring back at him, was the stunning proof that he'd taken a *virgin*.

Furious that he'd been played, tricked, he'd questioned his friend Daniel, Marquis de Gallay, the host of the masquerade. Made discreet inquiries everywhere. No one knew who the auburn-haired seductress was. For the longest time he'd been unsure whether he'd be hauled to the altar or called out. But the lady's family never stepped forward.

She'd left him with a sizzling memory and unanswered questions. Worse and even more maddening, after all these years she still made appearances in every one of his erotic dreams.

Was it possible that after five years he'd found the mysterious beauty who had sneaked into his chambers and awakened him with a searing kiss?

Adrien stalked to the door, reaching it in an instant, and snatched it open.

"Well? Will you do it?" Charlotte called out. "Adrien? Where are you going?"

He crossed the threshold with purposeful strides.

*****

Moving through the gardens, Catherine walked arm in arm with Suzanne—her friend and former sister-in-law and the only good thing to come out of her brief scandal-ridden marriage. If Suzanne's guests were privy to gossip about Catherine's late husband, the Comte de Villecourt, they gave no indication of it.

Strains of music from the violins sweetened the summer air and blended with the trickling sounds of the fountains.

Her tension easing, Catherine was starting to enjoy herself. She'd remained in mourning two years—longer than her marriage had lasted—and had thereafter kept to herself at Château Villecourt, away from the gossipmongers who'd gleefully spread the sensational details leading to her late husband's fatal duel.

It was Suzanne who had convinced her to visit last year. It was Suzanne who'd introduced her to her present betrothed, Philbert, Comte de Baillet. And it was Suzanne who'd persuaded her to take this sojourn before her impending nuptials.

"You aren't really going to marry Baillet, that old bore, are you?" Suzanne asked, her hostess's smile affixed to her face as they moved past the guests.

Catherine's smile was genuine. "I am. I shall proudly be the Comtesse de Old Bore." Her laugh moved Suzanne to one as well.

Sobering, her friend remarked, "I know my brother made you suffer, Catherine. I only want your happiness."

Catherine arrested her steps. "I am happy. Philbert and I will get along fine." Philbert was not the most exciting of men, but she'd endured enough *excitement* to last a lifetime while married to Villecourt. Philbert was the right choice. She'd have a quiet existence, financial security, and that was enough to satisfy her. Shoving aside the twinge of regret, she silenced the small voice inside her heart that opposed the notion. It made no difference that he didn't love her. Or that she didn't love him. Such marriages were virtually unheard of. At least Philbert had enough regard for her to be discreet about any paramours he'd maintain.

Suzanne sighed. "I suppose . . . but . . . beneath that very proper exterior lies a vivacious woman. One desperate to get out. I fear the sheer dullness of the man will kill her."

"Suzanne—" Catherine's retort was interrupted.

"Madame de Lamotte!" a woman called out behind her. Turning, Catherine saw two women about her age briskly approaching.

"Ah, *Dieu* . . ." Suzanne murmured softly.

The two dark-haired females stopped before them, cheeks pink and slightly breathless.

"Is he here, madame? Has *le Beau* arrived?" blurted out Madame de Noisette the moment Suzanne had finished with the introductions.

"Yes, do tell," her friend Madame de Bussy, prompted.

"He is here." Suzanne's statement was weighty with a certain amount of smug pleasure.

Excitement bubbled out of the two women, the sound much like that of a gaggle of geese.

Catherine hid her amusement over their exuberant reactions. "Who is *le Beau?*" she inquired, her curiosity piqued.

Madame de Noisette's brown eyes widened. "You don't know *le Beau?*"

"I'm afraid I've never heard of him."

"Why, he's only the most handsome man in the realm," she explained. "He's one of the King's own bastard sons—Adrien, Marquis de Beaulain."

"And I hear he's between conquests," Madame de Bussy added. "His reputation as a master swordsman and"—she blushed—"in the boudoir is renowned. In fact, he's quite the celebrated libertine. All the women want him.'"

"Oh?" Catherine remarked, unimpressed.

Madame de Noisette tittered. "He's living up to the curse."

That grabbed Catherine's interest. *"Curse?"*

"Why, yes." Madame de Bussy looked around then stepped a little closer and continued *sotto voce*. "His mother was, for a time, the King's favorite. It is said that at le Beau's christening, one of the King's former favorites was overcome with jealousy, burst into the chapel, and cursed the child the moment the holy oil was placed upon his forehead."

Madame de Noisette shook her head. "Can you imagine such a thing?" Knowing how superstitious the King and his court were, Catherine understood the horror in the woman's tone. Uttering ill-intended words toward the babe was bad enough, but to hurl them at the anointing of the child was far worse. "Tell her what she said. Go on," Madame de Noisette urged her friend.

"Yes, of course . . . She said the babe would grow up to be exceptionally beautiful, charming, break women's hearts, as his father did, yet be *nothing but grief* to Louis. The King became instantly incensed at the woman. One of le Beau's godfathers, for his mother had three brothers and couldn't choose between them for such an honor, tried to mollify the King. As the story goes, he placed a hand upon the infant's crown and said that the child's looks and charm would indeed be great and that all would marvel at him. That he would fill His Majesty with pride, for a son so fine could only belong to the ruler himself."

Catherine glanced at Suzanne and caught her rolling her eyes.

"Really, madame, that tale has been retold too many times with too many variations to be believed," Suzanne said.

"It is true!" Madame de Bussy insisted, then turned to Catherine. "It's all come to pass. He most definitely has looks and charm, and at the age of majority, barely fifteen, he pricked his first woman."

Her friend laughed. "My dear, I believe you mean *he used his prick* for the first time to tumble a woman."

Madame de Bussy's face turned crimson again. "Ah, yes, yes, that is exactly what I mean. And he has been using that particular part of his anatomy to delight many fortunate females ever since." By the sparkle in her eyes, Catherine could tell Madame de Bussy was anxious to be his next conquest. Since most men preferred to live at their hôtels in Paris while their wives were banished to their country châteaus, the ladies before her could easily take a lover, as many did, without anyone being the wiser.

"And, my dear, let us not forget how often His Majesty has had to look the other way each time le Beau has broken his own father's law by duel—" Madame de Noisette's words froze on her tongue and her mouth fell agape as she stared beyond Catherine.

"It's him!" Madame de Bussy exclaimed.

Catherine was just about to turn around when Madame de Noisette grabbed her arm. "Don't! Don't turn around. He is looking this way and it will seem as though we are speaking about him."

"We are speaking about him, madame," Suzanne said blandly.

"Oh, my." Madame de Noisette removed her hand from Catherine's arm and pressed it to her bosom. "He is coming this way."

Suzanne was now facing her approaching guest with a welcoming smile.

Unable to resist a peek at the roué, Catherine peered over her shoulder. Her stomach dropped the moment her gaze locked on to a set of arresting green eyes. Sinfully seductive, intimately familiar light green eyes. Her limbs went cold and her knees felt suddenly weak.

Dear God, it's him . . .

"Hmmm? What did you say?" Suzanne asked, still focused on the ever-nearing le Beau.

"No, nothing." *Oh God. Oh God. Oh God. He's the bastard son of the King!* She'd tainted his wine with an aphrodisiac. He could have her arrested for that. For her rash—idiotic—act. Every fiber in her body screamed, *"Flee!"*

"Suzanne," she croaked out, her heart hammering.

Her friend dragged her gaze back to her, her smile instantly dissolving. "Catherine, are you all right? You're flushed."

"I've suddenly developed a terrible headache. I'm going to lie down. Excuse me." She fisted her skirts and made her way across the gardens, forcing herself to keep to a swift walk and not a full-out run. She maneuvered around the guests, never making eye contact, never turning around, using the bushes to shield her from le Beau's view whenever possible. Around the side of the château she'd find the servants' entrance.

Ten more feet and she'd be out of sight.

Her breaths were ragged.

Eight feet. *Hurry!*

How could Odette have been so mistaken? Her maid had told her that the beautiful stranger she'd spotted at the masquerade five years ago was a foreigner. From Vienna.

She rounded the side of the château. *At last . . .*

Tossing a quick glance over her shoulder, Catherine bolted for the wooden door, all but falling against it when she reached it. Briefly fumbling with the latch, she opened it, ducked inside, and raced through the kitchens, negotiating around each busy servant who got in her way, ignoring their curious looks. Smoke and the heavy scent of roasting meats assailed her nostrils and scorched her throat. *Move! Move! Get to your rooms!*

She rushed up the servants' darkened stairs and stopped at the door that led to the upstairs hallway. Cautiously, she opened it and peered out. Empty!

Only twenty feet remained between her and her chamber door. Wasting no time, she stepped into the long corridor and made her way to safety, her legs wobbly with each rapid step she took.

"Madame?" A male voice arrested her steps.

And her breathing.

She heard footsteps approaching.

Don't panic. It could be anyone. *Let it be anyone other than—* she turned. Her knees almost buckled.

Le Beau.

CHAPTER TWO

Where had he come from? The shadows? Likely the grand stairwell.

Two final strides and he was before her. Tall. Muscled. With hair the color of a moonless night sky. Her fingers began to tingle. Catherine clasped her hands tightly together. She could still feel its cool silky texture between her fingers, as if it were only yesterday that she'd caressed his dark hair. She'd forgotten just how large a man he was—his broad shoulders, his magnificently sculpted form. She felt small, very feminine near his powerfully built body.

Give nothing away. He doesn't remember you. He can't. Then why did he leave the gardens so quickly? Why is he here?

Schooling her features, she expelled the air from her lungs and met his gaze unwavering. "Yes?" she said, amazed at the coolness in her tone when she was on the brink of discomposure.

Those unforgettable light green eyes scrutinized her face. She fought not to fidget. His presence and proximity were disquieting on so many levels. Her insides quaked.

"I believe we've met, madame."

Her heart lurched. She managed a small smile. "I'm afraid you have mistaken me for someone else. Now, if you'll excuse me." She turned.

He caught her arm. A jolt of sensations shot through her.

"Unhand me," she said, shaken, a dizzying combination of excitement and dread inundating her.

He released her. Without a word, he walked around her slowly, his bold assessing gaze moving over her body. Taking in her every detail. She could feel his tactile regard right through her clothing, making her hot from the inside out.

"Sir, your conduct is outrageous." Did she sound as breathless as she felt? "You are being extremely rude."

He stopped, his towering form now a formidable obstacle between her and the door to her rooms.

"It's you," he said.

She swallowed and lifted her chin a notch. *"Pardon?"*

"You're the woman who sneaked into my chamber that night five years ago."

Stirring memories filled her mind. She shoved them aside as she'd done many times throughout the years.

"You are mad. I told you—I don't know you."

He tilted his head to one side, a smug look in his eyes, much like the cat that had cornered the mouse. "Madame, you do know me—in the biblical sense. Though there was nothing but sinful delights in what we shared."

Heat crept down her face and neck to her chest. "Tell me," she responded with as much calm as she could muster. "Is this a habit of yours? Skulking around hallways? Making lurid—unfounded—accusations?" she asked. "Or perhaps this is your twisted way of enticing women? By telling them of your sexual exploits. Are there women who actually fall for this ploy?"

He stepped closer. Awareness rippled through her. Yet she refused to step back, refusing to show that she was in any way intimidated by him. His mouth was oh, so close to her own . . . Images of that skillful mouth on her body, grazing over her skin, drawing on her breasts made her sex clench and moisten.

"Perhaps you and I have a different definition of *twisted*," he said. "I'd like to know what twisted motives you had when you decided to taint my wine and surrender your innocence to me."

"It sounds like you had quite an evening," she said without

flinching. "Though I can't comprehend why—after five years, did you say?—it would be so vivid in your mind. How can you be certain that it was I? Surely, you managed to find a woman or two since then willing to overlook your barbaric manners. You are"—she shrugged—"mildly attractive."

His brows shot up, surprised at first, then his lips twitched as he fought back a smile.

"Have I amused you?" How she wished he'd step back. His closeness was making it difficult to breathe. Or think. She had to get away from him. From the château.

Preempt her vacation.

"You have. I'm not accustomed to receiving a set-down from a woman." He slipped his fingers beneath her chin and caressed his thumb along her cheek. Pleasure streaked from his touch down to the tips of her breasts, causing her nipples to harden instantly.

She jumped back—a purely reflexive response—and bumped into the wall. He braced his palms on either side of her shoulders, trapping her.

"I am also not accustomed to having a woman dupe and drug me." He stared at her pointedly.

Catherine glanced at her chamber door. It was so close, yet it might as well have been on the other side of the country. She couldn't simply race to it and bolt the door behind her. That would only make matters worse.

You've got to convince him he's mistaken. Fail and he could have the King draw up arrest orders. They'd leave her to languish in prison—until her trial and certain execution. Other women had suffered this fate. Because of the recent poisonings at court, there was a heightened hysteria now. Administering *anything*, even something as harmless as a love potion, without the other person's knowledge was punishable under the law. No matter when it was done.

Adrien scrutinized the woman before him with the discerning eye of a libertine. Her skin was flushed and her breasts rose and fell with her quickened breaths in the most intoxicating, mouthwatering way. *Jésus-Christ*, that auburn hair, delectable form, and those brandy-colored eyes… She was just as alluring as he remembered.

He was *not* mistaken.

She was indeed his midnight temptress.

She knew it. He knew it. And so did his cock. She hadn't done anything more heated than to glare at him, yet she had him stiff as a spike, his hard prick straining against his breeches. The way her small pink tongue unconsciously licked her lips was driving him to distraction.

Her indignation was an act. She was trying to conceal not only the truth, but her arousal as well. Her nipples were hard and her frequent glances at his mouth were telling. Thoughts of taking her to her chamber, stripping her naked, and sinking his length into that tight juicy core of hers—of purging her from his system for good—were running rampant in his mind. *Merde*, there was no short supply of willing women. The last female he should want was one who'd schemed and stooped to such trickery. Unfortunately, his cock didn't agree with his head.

No woman had ever occupied his thoughts or dreams the way she had. And he resented it.

He resented that the best fuck of his life had been drug-induced.

She'd left him to imagine every possible scenario that had motivated her actions. With no way of confirming any of them. Now that he'd found her and knew her name, he wasn't going to relent. No matter how lovely she was, how enticing, how physically pleasurable that night had been, she *was* going to admit what she'd done and tell him *why*. He was going to have answers to the questions that had plagued him for years.

She owed him as much.

"Perhaps you are reluctant to discuss the matter because of who I am—or better yet—who my father is. But I assure you I want answers, not revenge," he said. It had to be a barrier for her. One he wanted out of the way to clear a path for the truth.

"I've nothing more to say to you, sir. This conversation is

over." She had an obstinate look in her eyes, one that said she wouldn't confess. That she'd never confess. It steeled his resolve. If she wanted to engage in a round of wits and wills, he'd play along. She'd started this game. He'd finish it. And win. It was time to chisel away at her façade.

Since it was clear she wasn't immune to him, he chose his course of action.

His palms still pressed against the wall, Adrien dipped his head. The light scent of jasmine inundated his senses with a heady rush. "Catherine . . ." he said softly in her ear, her edible little earlobe so temptingly close to his hungry mouth. "I've thought of that night many times." She placed her hands against his chest as if to stave him off but didn't push him away. Encouraged, he continued. "I remember the sweet taste of your mouth . . . your pink nipples . . . details of your beautiful body . . . You remember our night together. Having me inside you . . . as you came, again . . . and again . . ." She shivered with excitement. It reverberated inside him. His cock began to pulse. "*Ma belle*, admit it was you." He brushed his mouth over the sensitive spot under her ear. She made a strangled sound and turned her face away, inadvertently giving him better access to the slender column of her neck. Or perhaps it wasn't so inadvertent.

But stubbornly, she remained silent.

Urgency thundered through him. Her soft skin beckoned. He drew her warm skin between his lips and gently sucked. She fisted his shirt and gasped. Her pulse beneath his mouth was as wild as his own. She tasted of jasmine. And slightly salty. Sweet womanly sweat from her nervous excitement. "Tell me what I wish to know," he murmured. "And I just might give you what your body is begging for."

He moved to her earlobe and lightly bit it. This time she moaned, the delicious sound making his sac tighten and his heart hammer harder. She was too damned desirable. The crest of his cock was moist with pre-come, his body clamoring for him to take her right here against the wall.

He'd been with enough experienced women to know that she was not. In the last five years, she hadn't gained any significant experience. He couldn't believe this sexual novice had him this undone. Just as undone as he'd been five years ago when—in his ravenous state—he'd overlooked the signs of her innocence.

Pulling back slightly, he gazed at her face. She was panting, his breathing no less affected. She stared back at him. Her cheeks were pink and her lips were parted, begging to be kissed. Hers was no ordinary mouth. It was extraordinary—made to drive men wild.

Grappling with self-control, Adrien could barely moderate himself. "There is a way to put this to rest, you know. To prove once and for all whether or not you are the woman I seek."

Something flickered in her amber depths. Confusion? Curiosity?

"You see," he continued, "the woman who came to my bed that night had lovely breasts, much like yours . . . and on her left breast, right here"—he stroked his fingers along the outside curve of the soft mound, and she gave another delightful gasp— "she had three small freckles. A pretty constellation that, if connected, would make a perfect tiny triangle."

He thought he saw her flinch, though it was so slight, he wasn't certain he'd seen it at all. The sexual haze in her eyes dissolved. Replaced by a fire of a different sort.

She shoved his hand away. "Are you suggesting I show you my *breast?*" she said, clearly incredulous.

He pressed both palms against the wall once more, and tilted his head to one side, his mouth mere inches from hers. "It would prove whether or not you are my mystery lady. Come with me to my chambers or invite me to yours—someplace where we'll be more comfortable. I promise, you'll enjoy every moment." Her gaze once again dropped to his mouth. His greedy cock jerked in response. Adrien leaned in a little closer, their lips all but touching. "Which is your room, Catherine?" he whispered against her tempting lips. He was dying to possess them. He was dying to possess her.

"Adrien!" a male voice called out.

She squeaked, ducked down and slipped out from under his arm so quickly, he almost kissed the wall.

"Merde," he growled, shoving himself away from the wall. His head snapped around in the direction of the intruder, with every intention of venting his full fury over the interruption.

Merde. Merde. Merde! His three godfathers stalked toward him. What the bloody hell were they doing here?

Was everyone he was related to going to show up at the Comtesse's château?

He looked at Catherine. She'd paled and was using him as a shield from his approaching uncles. Her gorgeous eyes were large, beseeching, as if she thought he'd make the situation worse. They both knew that she'd been caught in a compromising situation with a man who had a shameless reputation.

He stepped in front of her to better conceal her from the ever-nearing trio. "Go quickly," he said over his shoulder.

Dainty footsteps rapidly retreated down the hall behind him and then a door closed just as his godfathers stopped before him.

Adrien clenched his teeth, his muscles taut, his body rioting for release. He was in sexual agony, *unnecessary* sexual agony, for given a few moments more and he'd have had the auburn-haired enchantress behind closed doors . . . "Before I ask you what you are doing here, I wish to tell you that your timing couldn't be worse."

"Or better—depending how you look at it," said Charles, the eldest of his three uncles.

"I don't know if I agree with that." Paul looked past Adrien. "I got a glimpse of her. I think I'd be rather distressed to miss out on a tumble with that mademoiselle." He grinned, and Robert laughed.

Charles simply scowled.

Though Charles had always been less of a skirt chaser than his two younger brothers, he was no saint. In short, Adrien had been raised by no fewer than three rakes. Not to mention, his father was the greatest womanizer by far. In truth, Adrien came by his rakish ways honestly.

"I, my brother, got better than a glimpse," Robert said. "Wasn't that Madame de Villecourt?"

A novel emotion clenched in Adrien's gut as he wondered how his libertine uncle knew Catherine. The emotion took him completely by surprise. He was not the possessive type. His dalliances were always brief, recreational, without any sort of emotional involvement whatsoever.

Charles's salt and pepper brows arched. "Madame de Villecourt? Are you certain?"

Robert gave a wolfish grin. "Indeed I am. Though I haven't seen her in years, I never forget a beauty like that." He looked pointedly at Charles. "She's just as beautiful as her late aunt was."

Charles scowled anew.

"So, Adrien, is the lady as fiery in bed as her hair would suggest?" Paul needled.

Adrien turned and marched down the hall, aggravated, frustrated, with a raging erection and his blasted godfathers on his heels. He wasn't about to relay any juicy details about Catherine, nor did he care to hear about Charles's likely conquest of Catherine's departed aunt.

Upon entering his rooms, he went straight to the brandy decanter on the ebony side table, and poured himself a liberal amount. He tossed it back and downed a second goblet before he was ready to engage with the three men before him.

Paul walked up to him and took the decanter out of his hand to fill his own goblet.

"My father sent you," Adrien stated.

Charles folded his arms. "He wants you at Versailles, Adrien."

"I've already told him no."

"Yes, and that answer isn't satisfactory to the King." Charles accepted a goblet of brandy from Paul.

Adrien held back the expletives thundering in his head, striving for calm. How was he to keep his distance from the man who'd wreaked such havoc in his life? Especially when he mixed parental authority with royal command.

He wanted nothing to do with Louis and his court. Every time his father reentered Adrien's world, he caused him anguish and suffering.

He'd done enough damage during Adrien's childhood.

His beloved mother had been born into nobility and widowed at a young age. Using her beauty, wit, and charm, she chose her lovers wisely, until she eventually caught the roving eye of Louis XIV. For a time, she held the coveted position of the King's favorite mistress. But his mother made one grievous error: she'd allowed herself to fall in love with her lover. Enamored as she was, she never shared Adrien's jaundiced opinion of his father. Even when she'd been replaced by another woman and sent to live with her brothers, she still clung to the hope of rekindling Louis's interest.

She'd anxiously awaited each infrequent visit.

Adrien had dreaded them.

Louis would stay long enough to pat him on the head and bed his mother. Then he'd be gone, leaving her bereft each and every time. Heartbroken, she eventually abandoned Adrien and Charlotte to their uncles and entered a convent.

Robert sat down near the hearth, accepting a goblet of the amber liquid from Paul. "Louis feels that living at Versailles will curb your wayward ways."

Adrien finally exploded into a string of oaths. "What wayward ways?"

"Asks the man who was just caught with a most alluring widow." Smiling, Paul sat down beside Robert on the settee.

Adrien tightened his jaw. He was in no mood for Paul's ribbing.

"Duels are against the law," Charles began.

Adrien raked his hand through his hair. "Not this again."

Charles pressed on. "The King has looked the other way each

time. Your hand is too quick to the scabbard."

"I've not fought a duel for over a year. Does that not satisfy him? Perhaps he disagrees with my paramours? Too few? Too many? Maybe he wishes me to join the Order of Malta? Does His Majesty want me to take the required vow of celibacy?"

"A vow of celibacy." Paul shuddered in horror. "Is there anything worse? Or more unnatural?"

"Adrien," said Robert, always the peacemaker, using his be-reasonable tone. "We know how you feel about your father—and with good reason—but he is the King. He has treated his children well—if not his mistresses."

"He has?" Adrien snorted. "I must have missed that day. When was that? It certainly didn't occur during my boyhood. Ah, yes, perhaps it was last year—just after my mother died. Fully aware of her passing, her body not yet cold in her grave, he demanded I attend the festivities at Versailles. Was that the day, Uncle? He'd shown her little regard during her life and couldn't even muster any for her—*or me*—after her death. *'The King abhors any talk of the dead. He doesn't tolerate any expression of grief,'* I was forewarned as I arrived. I spent two excruciating weeks, forced to smile and make merry, attend picnics and hunts, forbidden to mention my mother's name for *'it would sadden the King and His Majesty doesn't like to be melancholy.'* Was that one of the benevolent examples you're referring to?"

Charles hung his head. Robert rose from his seat, walked over to him, and placed a hand on his shoulder. "She was our sister. We feel your pain."

Did they really? Did they know the extent of his devastation as he watched his mother withdraw from him and Charlotte? All love and warmth slipping from her heart and demeanor until all that was left was a shell of her former self? He was eight when she'd informed him—cold and detached—that she was leaving. He'd wept. He'd begged her not to go. To no avail. At the convent, he'd thrown himself on the front steps, a pathetic childish attempt to stop her, his heartbreak evident in his anguished wails. He could still see her expressionless face as she clutched her skirts, stepped over him, and climbed the final steps to disappear behind the large wooden doors of the Convent of the Sacred Heart. Vanishing from his life.

Paul rose and approached. "He has removed the blemish of being illegitimate, elevating all of his children in society by providing each of you with lands and a title—"

Adrien slammed his goblet down on the side table and walked away from his uncles, feeling suddenly suffocated. Stopping before the window, he braced his hands on the wooden frame, silencing the agony welling inside him. He'd mastered the pain long ago. He never let it overwhelm him anymore. It was why he preferred to maintain a comfortable level of detachment in all relationships. Especially with women. Being in control both in and out of the boudoir was paramount. He limited the time he'd spend with each female and didn't allow feelings to be fostered—for either party. His encounters with women were about sex. Mutual pleasure in the moment. The women—utterly forgettable.

Except his midnight temptress.

The pretty little conniver, thanks to her potion, had robbed him of his control and branded him with a memory so heated, he couldn't vanquish it.

"I care nothing about the lands or title. I care not if he takes it all away."

"He knows that about you," Robert said.

"I won't live at Versailles. I'd sooner have him place me in the Bastille. I prefer that prison over the gilded one he has planned for me."

Robert sighed. "He knows that about you, too. That is why he sent us to reason with you. He doesn't wish to take such measures against his son."

Adrien turned. "*Jésus-Christ*, he has many 'sons.' And daughters, too. Why is he so focused on me?"

"Perhaps it is because you remind him of himself," Charles responded. "Everyone knows what little regard he has for his heir. The Grand Dauphin doesn't have the mental and emotional fortitude to take the throne. And though he will succeed him nonetheless, Louis has no respect for him. But you . . . you he respects."

Paul nodded. "Probably because you resist him, at times defy him, when others wouldn't dare."

He wasn't trying to be defiant. He was simply trying to encourage a parting of ways.

"At least consider joining him at court, Adrien," said Charles. "There are plenty of women there to entertain you. Please him, and he'll likely let you select your own bride, and offer a high-ranking position where you will—"

"Enough of that, Charles." Robert walked up to Adrien. "Adrien has already made it clear that none of that entices him." Robert turned to Adrien. "Stay here. A week. A month. Whatever you need. But do consider the matter carefully."

There was nothing to consider. He wasn't going to change his mind, and he was angry that his uncles were even asking this of him.

"Robert is right," Charles said. "Stay. Drink. Enjoy yourself—just don't do so with Madame de Villecourt."

"And why the hell not?" Paul asked for him.

Charles crossed his arms. "Because I heard, while at Versailles, that she is to marry Philbert, Comte de Baillet."

Paul waved a dismissive hand. "That makes no difference. Everyone poaches."

"The Comte de Baillet is a man Louis holds in high esteem. If Adrien chooses to deny his King's request—a colossal mistake, I might add," Charles said, "then I should think he wouldn't want to give his father more reasons to be annoyed with him—that is, if he wants to walk away unscathed."

His Majesty ruled by intimidation. If there was a way to force Adrien to comply, Louis would have done it. He wouldn't have sent his uncles to "reason" with him. Adrien *was* going to walk away unscathed. Louis wasn't going to strip him of his lands and title or have him arrested or do anything whatsoever to risk having anyone learn that his son had denied his request and hadn't cowered before the mighty Sun King. In Louis's mind, that would make him look weak. And that he would never do.

However, his father wasn't going to simply relent. He was going to quietly, incessantly try to break Adrien and get him to acquiesce.

No, if he wanted his father to be out of his life—free himself from his clutches—he'd have to press the matter further.

Philbert de Baillet was going to assist in that regard.

The man was an ass. He had no backbone to speak of. He'd never call Adrien out no matter what he did with Catherine. More important, Philbert had the ear of Louis's most pious wife, Madame de Maintenon. He'd run straight to her and lament about Adrien—as he had in the past whenever someone fell out of favor with him. Louis was absolute ruler on matters of state, but when it came to religious observation and devotion, he looked to Madame de Maintenon, his second wife. She'd greatly influenced a vice-ridden King and his court, curbing their ways.

Madame de Maintenon didn't think much of hedonists like Adrien.

She'd been cordial to him. Respectful of him the entire time he'd spent at Versailles, keeping her opinion of him to herself. But a dalliance with the future wife of someone she considered a dear friend would loosen the woman's tongue. It would likely convince her that Adrien was corrupt by nature, and therefore unredeemable. And she'd express to the King her vehement displeasure at having Adrien permanently at Versailles.

Madame de Maintenon and Philbert de Baillet were about to aid in his cause and become Adrien's unwittingly allies. As would the lovely Catherine.

He felt a smile tug at the corners of his mouth, pleased for the first time since this conversation began.

Charles's brow furrowed. "Why are you smiling?"

"Why, Uncle, you just made Catherine de Villecourt even more appealing."

Chapter Three

"Odette, we're leaving!" Catherine announced the moment she located her maid in her rooms, her insides still quivering.

Odette was holding two of Catherine's gowns, one over each arm. Her brown eyes widened. "But, madame, you've only just arrived. I was unpacking—" Catherine's belongings were spread across the bed.

"Gather everything. We must leave right now." She'd leave the country. Where could she go? She had virtually no money. Perhaps Suzanne could advance her some funds. *Dear God, he knows your name* . . . Her hands shaky, she snatched up one of her gowns off the mattress and tossed it back in her trunk, then turned grabbed another and tossed it in, too.

Perplexed, the older woman watched her haphazard packing. "What has happened? What is amiss?"

Catherine pulled the gowns from Odette's arms and tossed them into the trunk as well. "I'll tell you what is amiss. The gentleman whose wine you spiked five years ago is *here.*"

Odette's mouth fell agape. She clamped it shut and swallowed. *"He—He is?"*

"Yes, and that's not all. He isn't from Vienna. He's French."

Ashen, Odette sank into a nearby chair, looking suddenly older than her forty-nine years. *"He—He is?"*

"He is! And will you stop repeating that."

"Has he . . . seen you?"

"Oh, yes. He has seen me. And recognized me as being the woman who tainted his wine then gave herself to him."

Odette blinked. *"Oh, Dieu . . ."*

"Oh, and it gets better," Catherine continued. "Would you like to know who his father is?"

Odette wound her apron around her finger. "Well . . . to be quite honest, madame . . . *not really.*"

Catherine crossed her arms. "I shall tell you anyway."

"I feared as much," she mumbled to her lap.

"His father is well known. A rather important man. Perhaps you've heard of him? The. *King.*"

Nervous, Odette smoothed her hand over her hair and mustered the semblance of a smile. "Oh? And which King might that be? Some small nation somewhere far—"

"Of France."

"Oh. That King."

Catherine threw up her hands. "Odette, you told me he was from Vienna."

Odette rose. "It's what I heard," she defended, then stopped and thought for a moment. "Or was it Venice? No. No. No. It *was* Vienna. I'm certain." She scratched her head. "Well, someone at that masquerade was from Vienna."

Catherine placed her hands on her maid's shoulders. "Odette, please focus. The man we tricked that night was the Marquis de Beaulain. He is the King's son. And he is demanding answers. For tainting his burgundy, he could have me arrested. In light of the recent poisonings at court, I could be tossed in prison . . . You remember what they did to Madame de Brinvilliers and the others . . ." As Catherine spoke, Odette was staring at her neck in the most peculiar way, her brows knitted together. Catherine continued because most of what Odette did was peculiar. Over the years, she'd learned to ignore most things. "I've told him that he's mistaken, but he doesn't believe—" Catherine stopped when Odette began tilting her head to one side, then her body at the waist, her gaze still fixed on the side of Catherine's neck.

"Odette, what are you staring at?" Catherine released her maid's shoulders.

Odette righted herself and peered closely, then pulled back, a slow steady grin spreading across her mouth. "It would seem that Monsieur le Marquis was not altogether cross with you." She walked over to the table and picked up a hand mirror. "Your Marquis has been perhaps whispering sweet words in your ear— among other things?" She handed the mirror to Catherine.

Catherine brought it up to her neck and saw the glaring undeniable marking of a love bite just under her ear. It was her turn to sink into a chair, which she did with a groan.

Her forehead fell into her palm. "Can this day get any worse?" she bemoaned.

The heavens responded with a thunderclap, followed by a sudden heavy rain, torrents striking the windowpane.

Her head snapped up. "Oh, no . . ." She rose and moved to the window. Sheets of rain were pouring from the sky.

"It doesn't look as though we can leave," Odette said behind her. "The roads will soon be useless."

Was this penance for her misdeeds? For conspiring to drug an innocent man and relinquishing her virtue? She thought she'd already paid for her sins during the course of her marriage.

"By the love mark on your neck, madame, I don't think you have anything to fear from him. Clearly, his interest in you hasn't anything to do with having you arrested."

Catherine closed her eyes briefly. A fresh rush of warmth flooded her already heated body.

Oh, to feel his mouth on her again had been sublime.

It left her starved senses famished for more.

The bulge in his breeches practically undid her. His magnificent erection was impossible to ignore. She'd aroused him. No aphrodisiac needed. It was a dizzying notion.

The man was not only impressively endowed—she recalled every glorious inch—but he knew how to use that part of his male anatomy with mastery.

She couldn't believe he'd remembered so much about her. At

first she thought he was lying. That it was impossible for a man as beautiful as he, with as many females as he had flocking to him, to have such a clear memory of her.

But he had.

He'd even remembered her freckles.

It was amazing. Inflaming. It made her ache. The bud between her legs throbbed for his attention. She hadn't felt desire in so very long. Not since one incredible night in the arms of a beautiful stranger after a masquerade ball. She'd had no idea sexual pleasure could be so keen.

"Madame, if I may suggest, why not simply enjoy him—until your betrothed arrives at the end of the week?"

She turned to face Odette. "Have you not heard what I've said? What could happen to me should he decide to have orders drawn up against me?"

The older woman shrugged. "From what I see, the Marquis de Beaulain would likely keep his mouth shut about the tainting of his wine if he had some other way to occupy it." She smiled.

Catherine frowned. "And what about Philbert?"

"What about him? It isn't a first marriage for either of you. And he already has an heir. Neither of you is in love. Most husbands expect discretion, not loyalty."

Catherine walked over to the hearth and stared at the flickering flames. Her life had finally fallen into place. She'd help raise Philbert's children and perhaps even have a child of her very own. She'd given up on romantic notions of love a long time ago. Security and a peaceful existence were all she hoped for. Was she going to lose everything because of something she'd done five years ago? Because of a chance meeting with the man who had the ability to collapse the foundations of her world.

What if she went to le Beau? What if she explained why she'd done what she'd done? Would he understand?

What if you offered yourself to him and enjoyed him as Odette suggested?

Catherine tamped down the fluttering that erupted in her stomach. Too risky. She'd already attempted something daring five years ago and look how disastrously that had turned out. This was a matter of life and death. Hers. She had no reason to trust le Beau and confide in him.

She'd have to maintain her innocence against his claim, put on a believable performance that would convince him he was wrong about her, and then leave Suzanne's château as quickly as she could. Staying in her rooms the entire time and feigning an illness was out of the question. He'd know she was hiding from him. It would only confirm in his mind that he was right about her. *God only knows what he'd do then.*

No, she had to carry on until her betrothed arrived at the end of the week. She'd show le Beau that he didn't rattle her in any way.

Easier said than done, Catherine. Look at your shocking behavior in the hallway.

Another thunderclap resonated in the angry skies.

Trapped at the château with the most sinfully seductive man of the realm. How, by all that's holy, will you resist his overwhelming allure?

*****

Arresting his steps in the corridor, Adrien crossed his arms with a sigh the moment he heard Charlotte call out his name behind him.

He was in a hurry. There was an auburn-haired beauty he had every intention of intercepting before she made it to supper. He'd barely had time to bathe and change his clothing after his uncles had left his rooms.

Charlotte stopped before him. "You've had a good look at Catherine. Can I count on your help, Adrien? She's reasonably attractive, although I am prettier." Though her last remark was a statement, it was said with self-doubt.

How he wished Charlotte wasn't so much like their mother.

"*Ma chérie*, forget Philbert de Baillet. If you have to work this hard to hold on to him, then he isn't worthy of you. You are very pretty. You can easily have someone else." He wasn't about to tell Charlotte of his plans for Catherine and have her enthusiastic over a lost cause. Catherine had little to do with Baillet's indifference. Baillet had lost interest in Charlotte. Plain and simple. There was nothing she could do to recapture it. It was best Charlotte ended the affair before he did. She'd save face. Her pride. Moreover, her heart. His godfathers were in agreement with Adrien.

Baillet would only bring Charlotte heartbreak.

Charlotte's eyes filled with tears and her bottom lip began to tremble. "*Pleeeease*, Adrien." Tears slipped down her face. "You'll do it, won't you?"

How he hated it when she cried. He despised it as much as he'd despised his mother's tears. He shouldn't be softened by them. But instead of being firm, "I'll see" tumbled from his mouth.

Her face lit up. "You'll do it!" She threw her arms around him and kissed his cheek.

He frowned, pulling her arms from around his neck. "That's not what I said."

She still beamed. "You love me, Adrien, though I know it's difficult for you to say. I know you'll do this for me." She squealed in jubilation and clapped her small hands. "No woman can resist le Beau. You must hurry. Supper will begin soon. Catherine de Villecourt will be there." With that, she rushed away.

"Charlotte, wait." But she didn't stop or turn around. "I'm not promising anything." She'd disappeared around the corner before he'd finished his sentence.

Adrien gnashed his teeth and walked away, clearing his mind of everything, except the captivating Catherine. Ironic that she'd be his pawn when he'd once been hers. But first, she was going to admit to her misdeeds.

The next left turn in the corridor brought him to the door he sought.

Catherine's door.

He stopped across from it and waited. Anticipation mounted by the moment. Adrien took a deep breath and let it out. He actually felt ... nervous. He'd never been nervous around women. He hadn't even been nervous with his first woman. The reactions she elicited from him were astonishing.

The door opened. Catherine stepped out. *A vision in a royal blue gown.* His heart lost a beat.

Adrien stood transfixed, his cock thickening. Her breasts, exquisitely defined, were an inciting sight to behold. His eyes feasted on the soft skin above her décolletage, her delicate bare shoulders and her elegant neck adorned by several strands of pearls. A slight purplish mark just under her ear grabbed his attention. A love bite.

His mark on her.

The sight inflamed him further.

The moment she saw him, her body went rigid. The servant with her gasped.

Catherine dragged her gaze from him, turned and walked down the hall, regal as a queen, dismissing him as if he were a common hand. As vexing as she was, he had to admit she was refreshingly different from any female he'd ever known. Hers was not the sort of greeting he was accustomed to receiving from women. The fact that she was going to be a challenge spiked his interest tenfold.

"Catherine ..." He raced to her side, falling in step with her quickened pace. "I'd like a word with you."

"I have nothing to say to you except, go away." She kept her gaze straight ahead. "And stop addressing me in such a familiar manner," she added curtly. The older woman with her scurried along beside her casting him the occasional timid look, seemingly distressed if the way she chewed her bottom lip were any indication.

"I thought since we were well acquainted, you wouldn't mind," he said.

"We are not well acquainted. I don't know how many times I have to tell you—I've never met you before. We haven't even been introduced."

"Ah, well, I agree with your last statement. If it's an

introduction you require, allow me to introduce myself—"

"Please don't bother."

"I am Adrien d'Aspe, bastard son of Louis XIV, and yes, most of the rumors you've heard about me are true. But, of course, you know a good deal about me. You've made inquiries."

She shot him a sharp look without breaking her stride. "I most assuredly have *not* made inquiries. You have the women here atwitter. They openly speak of you. I don't care who you are . . . or, in fact, to know anything about you."

"Come now, Catherine, don't be difficult. Dismiss your servant. Allow me a private moment. I promise you'll not be late for supper."

She surprised him when she stopped abruptly. "Sir, you are deranged. I have no interest in anything you have to say. If you don't leave me alone, I'll be forced to tell our hostess about your deplorable comportment." She turned and stalked away.

Despite himself, he felt a smile tugging at the corners of his mouth. When she was all afire like that, her eyes took on the most seductive glow.

He caught up to her and her servant again and stepped in front of Catherine so quickly that she walked into him and would have fallen back had he not caught her arms.

A mixture of frustration and outrage erupted from her throat. She opened her mouth, likely to toss out a few hot words at him, but he placed his finger over her lips silencing her.

"Whatever your relationship to Suzanne may be, I can assure you she'll not ask me to leave. She's been begging me to fuck her for months."

Her eyes widened, obviously caught off guard by his blunt answer. He removed his finger from her mouth. How many times had he thought about those ruby lips? Fantasized about them? Of sliding his cock between them into the wet warmth of her mouth. In five years, he hadn't been able to forget those lips or the delicious kiss that awoke him that night.

Taking advantage of her unbalanced state, he clasped her

hand in his and stalked toward her rooms with her in tow.

"Madame! Madame . . . wh-what should I do?" the servant called out.

"If you don't let go of me, I'll scream," Catherine threatened.

"Go ahead." He reached her door, wrenched it open, and pulled her inside.

"*Madame . . . ?*"

"It's all right, Odette. I'll take care of this," she said, just before he shut the door. He'd called her on her bluff. She wasn't about to scream. Or make a scene. If she wasn't scheming, she was lying to him.

She was always playing games.

Well, he had a game for her. One that would overwhelm her senses, break down her resistance. Only, he wasn't going to resort to drugging her—as she had him. But he *was* going to take control—a control she'd snatched from him that night.

His game was one he'd mastered a long time ago—seduction.

She narrowed her eyes. "What do you want?"

He stepped closer. She stepped back into the door. A crack in her façade.

"I want you to scream," he reiterated, his tone matter-of-fact. "I'm going to make you come, and I want to hear you scream out your pleasure."

CHAPTER FOUR

"Pardon?" The word rushed out on a breath, Catherine's bravado vanishing. In its place was stunned disbelief, and—Adrien was certain—a quiver of excitement.

He was wrong. There *was* something honest about her. Sexual arousal. She was naturally sensuous. Made for passion.

She craved it—beneath the veneer of propriety.

So why was her experience so limited? She'd been married, and as beautiful as she was, she could easily have her choice of lovers. Then there was Philbert de Baillet. Hadn't he sampled any premarital delights? Marriage was the last thing on Adrien's mind, but if he were betrothed to a woman like Catherine, he would have bedded her long before the exchanging of the vows.

Adrien snaked his arm around Catherine's waist and pulled her to him tightly. She gasped. He threaded his fingers in her soft hair, resting his palm on the nape of her neck. His fever for her spiked the moment their bodies touched. His cock pressing against her belly was already pulsing painfully. What was it about this woman? She scintillated his senses with no effort at all.

"You asked what I wanted, Catherine. I want to have another go at you, without any aphrodisiacs involved. But first and foremost, I want your mouth."

He swooped in for a kiss, her jasmine-scented skin inebriating him. She fisted the material of his knee-length coat against his back but, thank God, didn't push him away. Instead, she made tiny sounds at the back of her throat each time he locked and relocked their mouths.

Her breathing was already erratic, inciting his own. Yet by the slight stiffness in her body, he knew she was warring with her desire, wanting to stop him as much as she wanted him to continue. He forced himself to slow down. To concentrate on her responses, keeping her enthralled so that she didn't pull away from him.

Adrien brushed his tongue against her lips, coaxing them apart, sliding his tongue inside her mouth, penetrating it, possessing her mouth the moment she complied with his sensual demand. He celebrated in her surrender. She tasted delicious. Even better than he remembered.

Her soft form melted against his body, dragging a groan up his throat. *Dieu*, he wanted her.

The instant he felt her hands relax and flatten against his back, he cupped her breast and grazed his thumb over the hardened nipple. She rewarded him with a sultry moan. Pinching the pebbled tip through her clothing, he had her writhing and arching hard against him.

Catherine's hands shot up his back and tangled in his hair, her kisses now frantic. She gave his tongue a long, sensuous suck that practically buckled his knees.

His heart pounding against his ribs, he plucked at the ribbon between her breasts, loosening the front of her gown. Just as he started to spread open the bodice, she grabbed his hand and mewed, "No . . ." in protest ever so faintly against his mouth. She'd guessed his intent—that he had more than just sexual interest in seeing her exposed breasts. There were three small freckles on the outer curve of her left breast that he wanted revealed.

She didn't.

Cursing his eagerness, he stilled his hand, fearful of shattering her sexual abandon altogether. "Shhh, I won't, *ma belle*." This was novel. He always had carte blanche in the boudoir. No one ever said no to anything he wanted. "We'll only do that which we both want," he quickly assured her and reclaimed her mouth, starved for more. Gripping her pert derrière, he pressed his thigh between her legs and against her sex with enough pressure over her clit to draw another gasp from her, bringing her focus back to the pleasure at hand, away from his blunder.

"I know what you want," he murmured against her mouth, and rubbed her clit with his thigh. She jumped. He broke the kiss and looked into her eyes. Her cheeks were flush, and she had that fiery glow in her eyes that had nothing to do with anger and everything to do with hot, fierce desire. "This is what you want, isn't it? It's what we both want, Catherine. You're going to come for me—so hard—"

She grabbed his face and thrust her tongue inside his mouth, cutting off his words, her lower body rocking erotically against his thigh. Sounds of her sharp short breaths, as her tongue tangled with his, stoked his lust. Decimated his control.

He pushed her up against the door and removed his thigh from between her legs. Lifting her voluminous skirts with urgent yanks, he at last reached her drawers and cupped her through the cloth of the *caleçons*, already damp with her juices.

He caressed her lightly. "You're wet for me, Catherine."

"Oh . . . God . . ." Her voice was shaky. She pressed against his palm, more seductive sounds emanating from her. Urging him further. He needed no encouragement. He was so hard, he felt dizzy. The intensity of his need was stunning.

"Open your legs wider." His voice was gruff. Using his foot, he widened her stance. "Stay like that." Adrien slid his fingers in the slit of the garment, through her moistened curls, grazing over her slick flesh. She was hot, dripping with desire, and moaning louder.

Slowly, he pushed a finger inside her, feeding her a knuckle at a time until he buried it completely. The silky wet heat clasped around his finger was mind-numbingly tight. His prick twitched with anticipation. He couldn't wait to sink his cock into her.

He eased his finger out and slid two back in. She whimpered, her head falling back against the door.

"You're soaking my hand. Your body is begging for more." Massaging her clit with his thumb, he pushed and pulled his fingers with a deep and steady rhythm. She squeezed her eyes shut, dug her fingers into his shoulders and bit her lip, trying to muffle her sounds of pleasure, her lovely breasts rising and falling rapidly. She looked gloriously wanton.

"You like this, don't you? It feels good, doesn't it?" he asked.

She gave him a shaky nod.

"Does it feel as good as it did five years ago?"

Maddeningly stubborn, she wouldn't answer.

"You know I know how to make it feel even better." He curled his buried fingers and rubbed that ultrasensitive spot inside her vaginal wall. She cried out at the sharp carnal sensation and bucked her hips at him, her soaked sex pouring more juices onto his hand.

"Should I stop?" Adrien stopped teasing the bud between her legs and lightened the pressure of his strokes on the sweet spot inside her sex, giving her just enough to keep her hungry, keen, and on the edge.

She rolled her head against the door, her eyes still closed. "No!"

"You want to come badly, don't you?"

She swallowed hard. "Yes . . ." The sound of her breathless voice tightened his groin.

"Look at me."

She opened her eyes.

"Tell me you want my cock inside you." He had to have her. He couldn't stand it a moment longer.

"I want . . . I need—"

"What do you want and need?"

She licked her lips. "You . . ."

"Adrien, I need your cock," he amended, barely able to speak. "Say it."

"I need your . . . cock . . . Adrien."

Though he'd heard those words before, hearing them from her lush mouth shot a bolt of lust through him that rocked him to the core. He pulled out his fingers. She shuddered against him. Clutching her skirts in one hand, he loosened her *caleçons* with the other and watched them slip down her thighs. The sight of the wet downy curls between her legs made his mouth water.

Adrien yanked open his breeches and freed his stiff prick. It felt harder and heavier than ever before. Glancing at Catherine, he noticed her gazing hungrily at his engorged cock. If he hadn't been so aroused, he would have smiled. Here was the real Catherine: a highly sensual woman naturally drawn to decadent delights.

Grabbing her hips, he captured her mouth in a fierce kiss and slid his shaft between the folds of her sex, coating it with her essence, making it slick for easy penetration. He was so far gone, he knew he wasn't going to be gentle. "This is what you need." He wedged the crest of his cock at her opening.

"*Yes . . .*" She panted. "*Hurry!*"

He drove his prick into her, possessing her with a single thrust. She cried out.

Adrien closed his eyes and rested his forehead against the door, his chest heaving. Her hot slick sheath was stretched so tightly around him it made his cock throb, the pleasure pulsing along his length momentarily rendering him speechless.

Pinned against the door, impaled on his shaft, she trembled. He felt her tighten her arms around him, her warm fast breaths tickling his neck.

"I need your cock," she whispered near his ear.

That undid him.

He reared and thrust again. And again. And again. The friction felt so good. She felt so good. She had the sweetest sex. It was to die for. Vaguely, he heard her gasps and moans over the blood roaring in his ears.

She shoved her hips forward, taking fully each solid thrust he gave her. "Don't stop . . . Don't stop . . ." she pleaded each time he slammed into her.

As if he could? As if he had the will? "Tell me you're my midnight enchantress." His voice was so rough, it didn't even sound like his own. "Tell me . . . what I want to hear, Catherine . . . Tell me . . . you're the woman who came to my bed that night and I'll let you com—"

She screamed, her body jerking sharply as her orgasm slammed into her, taking them both by surprise, her inner muscles squeezing and releasing around his thick cock, milking his thrusting shaft with each powerful spasm.

Digging his fingers into her soft bottom, Adrien clenched his teeth and growled her name. Exquisite contractions rippling along his prick went on, and—*Christ*—on. He drove into her repeatedly, fiercely fighting back his orgasm to bask in her incredible cunt as long as he could.

How many times had he dreamed of this? Of having this woman again. Of sampling more of the scalding desire they'd shared. She was rapture incarnate. No aphrodisiac was necessary between them, and somehow he'd known it all along.

Her sex clenched around him a final time, snapping his flimsy control, his climax suddenly rushing over him. He jerked his prick out of her at the last moment, snatched her from against the door and crushed her in his arms just as his explosive release rocked him, his semen shooting out of him in deeply draining torrents. His mouth against her shoulder, he let out a long fierce groan, his body shuddering with each spurt of come until he'd emptied his cock.

His legs felt weak. His body lax. Ecstasy hummed in his veins. Memories of their last encounter, years ago, materialized in his mind. It had been exactly the same—soul-satisfying sex.

The night when you unwittingly took a virgin.

The sexual fog dissipating little by little, he became aware of his harsh breathing, the light scent of jasmine that hung in the air and her soft breasts crushed against his chest.

Adrien eased his hold on her. She slumped against the door. Her eyes were closed, her lips slightly parted. She had the prettiest blush to her cheeks. He brushed back a lock of her hair from her delicate brow. She looked like a woman who'd been well fucked and thoroughly sated.

A smile lifted the corner of his mouth. He took a small step back and glanced on the floor. His come was on her fallen drawers. Adrien kicked them out of the way, and wiping his glistening cock with his shirttails, he readjusted his clothing. Unlike his father, he took care not to make bastards.

Catherine opened her eyes. At first she looked away, seemingly embarrassed, but then she straightened her spine and met his gaze.

Lightly, he caressed her cheek with his knuckles. How he loved the feel of her skin.

Adrien felt mellow. He felt oddly content. He felt good.

No, he felt great.

"I've made a mess of your *caleçons*," he said. Not to mention he'd mussed her lovely hair and horribly wrinkled her gown.

"It doesn't matter." Her voice was soft.

His smile grew, pleased that she wasn't put off.

She cleared her throat. "Thank you for the . . . tumble." She slid out from between him and the door and stepped away, her gown falling into place. "Please see yourself out."

Adrien felt as though cold water just splashed him in the face. *Jésus-Christ*, she'd dismissed him. As though he were a stud for hire.

She didn't get more than two steps away from him when he caught her arm. Her head snapped around. "We're not through." His ire mounted.

Her fury flashed in her eyes. "You got what you wanted. Let go."

Stepping closer, he captured her chin and her undivided attention. She'd erected a wall between them again, and donned a false mask to conceal herself from him. He wanted it torn down. Stripped away. Wanted her naked both literally and figuratively. He wanted the truth.

Moreover, and most irritating, he wanted to know everything about her. And he had no idea why he should be interested.

"Catherine de Villecourt, you haven't come close to giving me what I want. But you will. We have only just begun."

Thunder rumbled in the sky.

CHAPTER FIVE

Hundreds of candles shone tiny stars of light in the *Salle de Buffet*. Wall sconces and the silver candelabras on the long table illuminated the room with a warm orange glow.

Ladies' gowns and gentlemen's justacorps of rich blues and greens, of deep gold and reds, lent to the opulence of the surroundings.

Catherine tried to concentrate on her conversation with the Comte de Champagnier. Seated to her right, the man had the most unfortunate monotone voice. It didn't help that his take on the Latin classics was uninspiring. Though only a few years older than she, he was incredibly dull. An avid reader, Catherine would have enjoyed a lively debate. Welcomed the much-needed distraction. Instead, the Comte's comments often blended into the din of the room. She smiled politely and made the occasional brief remark—brief because it was clear Champagnier was more interested in voicing his opinions than in hearing hers.

She didn't have anyone more interesting to talk to on her left. The ancient Madame de Jauloux was already chin-down, softly snoring before the meal was even served.

Catherine was stuck with Champagnier.

Her heart pounded away the time, knowing Adrien would arrive for supper at any moment. The room was full. Every seat was taken except the chair at the head of the table, which naturally Suzanne would occupy, and the one to its right.

Suzanne had likely arranged for Adrien to sit there, a spot that was across from Catherine and over two.

In short, uncomfortably close.

Shaken by their stunning encounter, she'd stopped trembling only minutes before entering the room. After what his kisses and touch had done to her, after her heated surrender in his arms, how would she get through the meal with him sitting so near? Her actions still had her reeling.

A few squeaks of delight and a rush of whispers rippled in the room, grabbing Catherine's attention.

Her heart lurched at the sight of Adrien standing in the doorway, Suzanne on his arm. He, too, had changed his attire. Now, he was dressed in a silver-green justacorps with matching breeches. He looked regal, princely, the knee-length fitted coat accentuating his broad shoulders and muscled physique perfectly.

He scanned the room. Those light green eyes—the downfall of many women—were a devastating contrast to his dark hair, wisps of which teased his lashes.

No man should be that beautiful.

She felt mortifying moisture pool between her legs. The very sight of him quickened her heart and ignited her senses— inspiring ardent thoughts and shameless urges no other man ever had.

Adrien escorted Suzanne to the table. Her dark hair was adorned with tiny ribbons that matched the row of green satin bows down the front of her bodice. Her gown, the height of fashion, was embellished with gold embroidery over alternate green and gold bands of satin. When her husband was alive, Suzanne didn't own such finery. Nor did the château look as it did now. Over the years since Comte de Lamotte's death, her wise selection of lovers had filled the once modest coffers. Hopelessly riveted, Catherine watched as Adrien whispered in Suzanne's ear. She glanced at Catherine as he spoke, her smile slightly slipping.

Catherine pulled her gaze away from the elegant couple.

"Monsieur de Champagnier," she said, returning her attention to the Comte. He, too, watched Adrien and Suzanne—as did the rest of the room. "Tell me, what do you think of Spanish literature? Have you any favorites?" That should have the man talking again, and give her something else—albeit ever so arduous—to focus on.

Champagnier began his prattle immediately, his flow of words arrested when a strong masculine hand gripped his shoulder.

Catherine glanced up. Her breath lodged in her throat. The hand belonged to Adrien.

"Good evening, Monsieur de Champagnier." Adrien's tone was genial, his manner polished.

Champagnier twisted around. "Good evening to you, Monsieur de Beaulain."

"There's a small problem, monsieur. It seems you're in my seat."

Catherine's stomach flip-flopped.

Champagnier brow furrowed slightly. "Monsieur, I'm afraid you're mistaken. The seats were assigned and—"

"Yours is over there." Adrien gave a nod to the empty chair near the head of the table, his tone firmer, though still pleasant. He lowered his head and his voice. "Do be a good man and take your place across the table without further ado. Unless, of course, you wish to make an issue of the matter?" A threat.

A few shades paler, Champagnier excused himself, murmured his apologies and vacated his chair. Being outranked hadn't motivated Champagnier to move, but the possibility of facing Adrien in a duel clearly had.

Catherine's gaze darted down the table. Her heart plummeted. Every eye in the room was on them.

"Cher," Suzanne said, placing a hand on Adrien's arm. Dear God, she hadn't even noticed Suzanne standing there. "Allow me to introduce my darling friend, Catherine de Sanvais, Comtesse de Villecourt. Catherine, this is Adrien d'Aspe de Bourbon, Marquis de Beaulain."

Adrien took her hand and pressed a kiss to her knuckle. "*Enchanté.*"

The ludicrousness of the moment struck her. She was being introduced to the man who'd deflowered her and, not an hour ago, debauched her. Catherine might have laughed if she wasn't so horrified.

"Madame de Villecourt was married to my late brother," Suzanne offered. "He passed away three years ago."

"Really?" Adrien's green eyes turned to Catherine, his expression unreadable, his vexation with her outwardly concealed. "My condolences, madame." He bowed at the waist.

Her heart pounding, she mustered a murmur of thanks.

"Enjoy," Suzanne said, looking at Catherine, before she swept to her seat.

Adrien sat down next to her.

Catherine cast another glance down the table. It wasn't difficult to note the looks. The whispers. They were talking about Adrien. About her. About them. Adrien was the closest thing to royalty in the room. Not to mention a source of interest to the aristocracy at large. Everything he did was noted and analyzed. Curiosity had gripped Suzanne's guests as they likely speculated at Catherine's involvement with the King's roué son.

Outwardly, she gave nothing away. Beneath the table, she clenched her hands together. During her excruciating eighteen-month marriage, she'd been the subject of gossip. The object of scandal.

The last thing she wanted was more of the same.

Platters with steaming meats were brought out by a parade of servants. Adrien's thigh brushed hers as he exchanged pleasantries with the Baron de Neveux on his right. She flinched and tried her best to ignore him and the tingling in her leg where their bodies had touched. She turned to Madame de Jauloux, who was now awake and watching the arrival of the food eagerly.

"Why, madame, that's a lovely necklace," Catherine said.

"Don't bother." Adrien picked up his goblet. "The woman is stone deaf. Aren't you, Madame de Jauloux?" he added a little louder.

She didn't appear to hear Adrien at all.

"You see?" he said. His eyes briefly dipped to Catherine's décolletage as he brought the goblet to his lips. Her nipples hardened. "You look lovely, Catherine."

Catherine squeezed her fingers a little tighter. "Please don't speak to me." *Or look at me like that.*

Adrien took a drink and placed his goblet back down. "Why not? We've been properly introduced." Despite the desire in his eyes, she sensed his underlying ire.

"You know exactly why not. Thanks to your spectacle, you have everyone wondering whether or not—"

"I'm fucking you?"

Nervous, she glance about, her cheeks feeling hot. Immersed in conversation, thankfully no one seemed to have heard him. Madame de Jauloux was happily engrossed in her poached egg soup.

Catherine clenched her teeth. Oh, she was definitely paying for her misdeeds this night. All of them. Including what she'd done with the devilishly handsome le Beau a short time ago. How much worse was this evening going to get?

Before she could offer a retort, a bowl of soup was set before her, her stomach instantly balking at the thought of food.

Adrien leaned into her slightly. Too close for her sanity. In fact, being in the same room with him was proving to be too much. "Why do you care what they think? Why should any of these people matter enough to you to waste a moment's thought on them?"

Catherine noticed Madame de Bussy and Madame de Noisette—the ladies she'd met in the gardens —openly observing her. Cordially, she nodded at them. "You are a man," she said with a frozen smile for the sake of outward appearances. "You are judged differently than a woman."

He shrugged. "I don't allow anyone's judgment—of any kind—to affect how I live my life and neither should you."

"Not everyone can afford to be as blasé."

Warm fingers closed over her cold hands beneath the table linen. She jerked.

"Easy." He lightly squeezed, his thumb grazing the back of her hand. A quick look told her no one noticed that his hand was on her lap. She couldn't pull away. He had her trapped, for any sudden movements would likely garner unwanted attention. His hand was so close to her sex, she could feel herself getting wetter.

Clearly, he was going to torment her on many levels. Her ire spiked.

"You are playing with me. All of this is a game to you," she shot back, *sotto voce*, furious with herself over the situation she found herself in. Frustrated with his effect on her. This entire mess was her fault.

"On the contrary, it is a game you play. You could be honest and tell me the truth. In truth, your desire is the only thing that's honest about you. It's the only thing that's honest between us." He brought her hand to the bulge in his breeches. Her heart lost a beat. He ran her hand down his length then back up. "It's what you do to me . . . just sitting near you."

The bud between her legs began to throb. She fought back the urge to tighten her grip on his glorious cock.

Adrien held up his goblet with his free hand. A server was there in an instant to fill it up with wine.

Did the servant not see? Catherine scanned the guests again. Didn't anyone notice what was happening under the table linen?

"I'll not denounce you," he said when the servant stepped away. "Whatever your reasons were for doing what you did five years ago, I'll not report it."

"Let go," she demanded quietly. Their eyes locked and held. For a moment she thought he was going to refuse, but then he loosened his hold, still keeping his palm lightly pressed against her hand.

She slipped her hand out of its tantalizing spot, sliding it away from his erection.

Taking in a fortifying breath, she let it out slowly, and chose her next words carefully. "Why, if a woman is faced with trial and possible execution, should she believe you? There would be a lot at stake for her in bestowing that trust."

He gave a nod. "True. But it's a matter that would be brought to the attention of the King, and I prefer to limit my dealings with His Majesty," he said. "Ask anyone. I have a strained relationship with my sire."

The "curse" Madame de Bussy had mentioned earlier flitted through Catherine's mind. Had the silly thing actually come true? It certainly sounded as though father and son were at odds.

Adrien leaned in again, his incredible green eyes disarming. "No one knows about that night except me and the host of the masquerade. He's a good friend. Most discreet. If you were I, would you not have the same questions I have? Would you not feel you deserved answers to them?"

That hit its mark. She lowered her head, feeling contrite. How could she argue with that? He did deserve answers. He had every right to them. He had every right to be angry with her, too, and yet he never once hurled vicious words as her husband used to whenever he was irked, which was more often than not. And then there was Adrien's touch. Whenever he touched her, it was always with genuine passion. It was beguiling. It made her feel feminine. Desirable.

An idea came to her. There *was* a way out of this after all—a way where everyone would benefit and no one would suffer. She decided she'd take a different approach to the matter. Hope welled inside her.

Catherine spied three men at the end of the table watching her. Two were smiling, almost grinning, while the third frowned.

"Do you know those men at the end of the table?" she asked.

Adrien's gaze moved down the row of seated guests. Then he frowned. "Ignore them."

"Who are they?"

Reaching for his goblet, he drained it. "My uncles. They are harmless."

"I don't want any scandal, Adrien. I've had more than my

share."

He studied her silently. "Oh?"

She arched her brows. "Surely, you've asked about me? Didn't someone tell you about my late husband?"

"No. I made no inquiries. I don't care for gossip. Nor do I want to learn about you from someone else. I want to learn about you, from you."

Catherine was speechless. She didn't know anyone who didn't partake in gossip—men or women. Some more viciously than others. It was refreshing to find someone else who shared her disdain for it.

Music started up in the Grand Salon, the harpsichord and violins playing a *menuet*. Catherine tore her gaze from Adrien's handsome face and noticed that already guests were moving to the next room. Adrien's uncles were also leaving, a pretty dark-haired woman exiting with them. Briefly, the woman met Catherine's gaze. A venomous look flashed in her hazel eyes so quickly, she wasn't certain if she'd imagined it.

A banquet of roasted duck, partridge and quails, fruits, salads, and pastries was spread out before her. Though most everyone had had their fill, none held any appeal for Catherine. Least of all her cold soup that she'd neglected to wave away.

She returned her attention to Adrien. He was watching her. All that masculine beauty focused solely on her. Her insides danced.

"I don't wish to speak here," she said. "I'll come to your room tonight."

"No. Wait out a few dances then retire to your rooms. I'll come to you."

"Very well. As long as you promise not to do anything to cause tongues to wag here."

"Agreed. And you'll agree to provide answers."

She nodded. "I'll have answers for you." And a bargain to sweeten the deal and ensure his silence.

*****

"Adrien," Paul said as he approached with a smile. "You'll soon bore holes in the Marquis de Verdier's back with the look you're giving him. Could it be it's because he's dancing with your lady?"

Adrien tightened his jaw. The moment Catherine entered the Grand Salon, she was besieged with offers to dance. This was her third dance already. Her radiant smile was telling. She was clearly enjoying the *allemande*, bewitching every one of her dance partners as they left looking smitten.

"She is not my lady," Adrien said, surprised by the twinge of regret.

"Why are you not dancing with her yourself?"

Why indeed? Why on earth had he agreed to keep his distance and not make their involvement more evident? *You know why.* It was something he'd seen in her eyes. A sorrow that stirred his compassion.

Instinct cautioned him against such sentiment, warning him not to be drawn in. Something told him that perhaps he should back off—that it might be best if he didn't learn the reasons behind her actions five years ago after all.

But as he watched her turn and curtsy, the final notes fading away to end the dance, he silenced the niggling doubts.

He knew nothing could keep him from her room tonight.

CHAPTER SIX

Pacing in her rooms, Catherine stopped dead in her tracks when she heard the expected knock at the door.

Adrien.

The moment of truth had arrived.

She'd promised him answers. The question was: what would he think of her answers?

Nervously she smoothed her skirts and opened the door. Adrien was leaning against the doorframe with his forearm. As usual, his presence sent a thrill through her.

She stepped aside, allowing him to enter.

"Please sit." She indicated the settee near the hearth in the antechamber.

He moved across the room, all muscle and masculine grace, and sat down, his rapt attention on her. Grappling with how to begin, Catherine clasped her hands, then released them and smoothed her skirts again. She'd practiced the words. But they were stuck on her tongue.

Adrien rose and approached her, his brow furrowed. Her nerves jangled; she braced herself, unsure what he was about to do or say.

To her surprise, he cupped her cheek. "Are you all right?" he asked.

It unbalanced her. She wasn't expecting him to be concerned about her emotional state. Her father and husband never were.

She'd learned to stand strong on her own long ago. To lean on no one.

Feeling vulnerable was unsettling in the extreme.

"You can trust me," he told her.

Did she have a choice? She'd failed miserably to convince him he was mistaken. He could have her arrested at any time. The freckles on her breast would ultimately condemn her.

She'd have to find the courage to open herself up to him and pray for the best.

Adrien saw fear in her eyes. She was clearly skittish. If he didn't proceed slowly, she'd likely bolt for the door.

He didn't want her to be afraid. Oddly, he found himself longing for her trust as strongly as he longed for the truth.

Something in the corner of the room caught his eye. An artist's easel and paintings propped against the wall. He moved toward them. On the easel was a lovely depiction of a valley at sunrise. It was serene. Lush. Beautiful.

"Did you do this?" he asked, marveling at the piece.

She moved to his side and blushed. "It isn't finished. It isn't very good . . ." she replied, quickly dismissing her work.

He leaned in closer to the painting and silently scrutinized it. "I think it's wonderful."

The initial look of surprise on her face was precious, as was the joy his praise gave her. It delighted him to see it more than he'd admit.

He motioned to the paintings on the floor leaning against the wall. "May I?"

She bit her lip, and after a moment's hesitation, gave a nod.

He picked up the paintings one by one and studied them, genuinely impressed. Paintings of gardens, of children, and one of water nymphs were among the works.

"You're very talented, Catherine," he said with all sincerity.

She looked embarrassed by his compliment. "Thank you. That's very kind of you to say, but . . . I'm rather an amateur . . ."

Her modesty was endearing. "Do you do portraits?" This was a first for him. He was alone with a beautiful, passionate female, his cock fully alert to her presence, and yet he wasn't acting on the powerful urgings she inspired.

"I've never really tried . . . My late father and husband both thought painting was a frivolous expenditure of time, especially for a woman."

"But you don't. You love it," he stated. "It's evident in these paintings. In the painstaking details. Each stroke of your paintbrush brought you joy, no?"

A smile returned to her lovely visage. "Yes. I do love it," she admitted softly. *Dieu*, this softer side of her was oh so appealing. The woman was beyond alluring.

"Excellent. Then you'll paint my portrait and one for each of my uncles," he said, ignoring the warning in his head against lengthening his involvement with her.

Her eyes widened.

"I'll, of course, pay for supplies," he continued, enjoying the astonishment on her face, "and for your—"

"I can't."

"Oh? Why not?"

She turned and walked over to the settee. Her back to him, he saw the stiffness in her delicate shoulders. "I'm to be married soon to the Comte de Baillet." She faced him. "He'll be here by the end of the week." Her statement added to the distance she'd just placed between them.

Adrien's dislike for Baillet grew each time he heard the man's name.

"I'm certain you think I'm rather shameless . . ." she said, her words trailing off.

She was still skirting around the issue, discussing matters other than the events that occurred five years ago.

Adrien closed the space between them and took her hand. "I don't think that." Lightly, he caressed her wrist with his thumb, relishing in the satiny feel of her jasmine-scented skin.

She didn't pull her hand away and it pleased him. Her expression was open. Unguarded. And that pleased him as well.

"What happened today . . . between us . . . I never intended something like that to happen," she said.

He didn't want her voicing any regrets. "We're attracted to each other, *ma belle*. Intensely so. There's no shame in that."

A small smile graced her lips. "You can be quite irresistible, but I'm certain you've heard that enough times."

"I've also heard I'm mildly attractive," he teased, pleased she didn't seem to be remorseful.

She laughed, a soft sweet sound. "If no one tries to keep you in check, dear Marquis de Beaulain, you'll become unbearably conceited."

"Well then." He bowed over her hand. "Madame, I thank you for your efforts. I'd hate to become intolerable." He kept the mood light though a new all-too-insistent question was now plaguing him, gnawing away at his brain.

Smiling, she shook her head. "You're incorrigible. But definitely charming."

"Then all hope for me is not lost." He brought her hand up to his lips and kissed the sensitive spot on the inside of her wrist.

Her smile faded, and she pulled her hand away. Adrien fought back the urge to take it again.

"Do you love him?" He was stunned at himself. The question eating at him just tumbled out of his mouth. He hadn't intended to ask. It shouldn't matter a whit if she did.

"My betrothed?"

"Yes." The last thing he wanted to hear from her were the same ill-placed words of adoration for Baillet his sister had.

To his relief, she shook her head. "No. Nor is he in love with me."

"Why are you marrying him?"

"After my father's death, Villecourt gained control of my inheritance."

"And squandered it," he surmised.

She looked down. "Yes. He had . . . extravagant ways. I find myself in dire straits. The château is in a state of ill-repair. I've had to let most of the servants go."

There was more about her marriage she wasn't saying. She'd

mentioned something about a scandal. But none of that was any of his concern. He wouldn't inject himself into her troubles. It wasn't why he was here.

Adrien slipped his arm around her waist and drew her to him, her soft form molding against him ever so delectably. Lust licked up his spine.

"Catherine, tell me what happened five years ago."

Suddenly unable to look him in the eye, she dropped her gaze to his chest. She was vacillating. Concerned she'd renege on her promise, he pressed on, untying the ribbon between her breasts, making quick work of the fastenings on her bodice with his practiced fingers before panic flared in her eyes and her hand shot up, stilling his with a firm squeeze.

He leaned in, the scent of jasmine dazzling his senses. "It's all right," he said softly in her ear. "Trust me. Let's put an end to the denials and lies. I only want the truth." He pulled back to gaze at her face.

She wouldn't look at him, her body rigid in his arms. Her hand still clutched his tightly.

"Let me," he urged gently. "On my word, it will be all right."

Keeping her gaze averted, she released her hold of his hand slowly.

Adrien opened her bodice and eased down her chemise, uncovering her skin an inch at a time until at last he located the three tiny freckles on the outside curve of her breast. There they were—those pretty freckles that had tantalized and tormented him in so many dreams. He caressed them with a finger.

Seeing them again triggered a rush of memories that weren't only heated. There was something else about that night that made her unforgettable, the experience unique. More than the intensity of it. More than the discoveries he'd made the next morning.

It was the tenderness.

Somehow she'd infused a certain softness into their carnal encounter.

Interwoven with the salaciousness, there was tenderness in

her touch. In her kisses. She'd taken what was supposed to be an anonymous fuck and made it far more intimate. Strikingly different. And most disconcerting—simply by how deeply satisfying it all was.

Taking several steps back, she readjusted her chemise, then covered her breasts with her arms.

She could pull away from him, but she couldn't backtrack now that he'd seen the freckles. "No more denials," he repeated. "It's time for explanations, Catherine. Why don't you start by telling me how you gained admittance into the masquerade? The guest list was rather exclusive. Daniel de Gallay swore to me that he didn't invite anyone fitting your description."

She paused. "The invitation was delivered to our townhouse in error. It was meant for our neighbor, the Comte de Quantin."

"You know Quantin? You lived on Place Royale in Paris?" It was relatively new, an elegant stretch of homes for the privileged.

"Yes. Once. The townhouse is long gone now." There was sadness in her tone.

"Thanks to your late husband?"

She nodded. "He lost it in a game of *Basset*."

"You used Quantin's invitation, then."

"No. I created a copy before I had one of the servants deliver it to the Comte."

"Why the strong desire to attend?"

Tears shone in her eyes, but she didn't shed them. "I was desperate. Why else would I go to the trouble of forging an invitation and sneaking out of my home?" She rubbed her arms, as though she were cold. "My family had made its fortune collecting taxes for the Crown. Father was determined to elevate our family into nobility through marriage. I was the sacrificial lamb. To that end, he chose the Comte de Villecourt as my husband." A rueful smile formed on her lips. "I wish I could have mustered some affection for him. I wanted to like him. Perhaps it sounds hopelessly romantic, but I truly wanted to fall in love with him. I held out hope, until I met him."

"What was he like?" he asked quietly.

She swallowed hard. Clearly, she was battling her emotions, trying to maintain her composure. He'd never known any female to hold back her tears. It was yet another reason why she stood out from the masses.

"He was . . . angry," she said.

Adrien's stomach tightened. "Did he ever . . . hurt you?"

"He never struck me, if that is what you mean. He tried to hurt me with words, but over time, I became numb to them. It was then he found different ways to torment me."

"Why would he wish to?"

She clutched her bodice to her bosom. "Villecourt was very much against marrying me to begin with. A bourgeois was far beneath him—a fact he never let me forget. He hated it that he'd had to accept me as a wife simply to replenish his family's coffers. We saw each other three times during our betrothal. He made no attempt to hide his disdain. He told me that if he had to suffer me as a wife, he'd make sure I was equally miserable. I begged Father to cancel the marriage contract. To reconsider and look for another. He refused. I knew I would live in sheer misery if I married Villecourt. It all felt so hopeless . . . and then the invitation arrived. I took it as a sign. A chance to escape my horrible fate."

The pain in her golden eyes wrapped itself around Adrien's heart even when he didn't want it to. "So, you decided to attend the masquerade to—"

"Purposely render myself unmarriageable. I'm sorry for what I did to you, Adrien. I'm sorry for whatever distress I caused you. If it's any consolation, my plan failed horribly and caused me further suffering in the end. It didn't break my betrothal, as I'd hoped. A larger dowry than originally promised mollified Villecourt's debt-ridden family's objections to my sullied state. As for Villecourt, it only fueled his resentment and made him more spiteful toward me."

Adrien was amazed. He had considered this scenario a possibility, and dismissed it. A maidenhead was a commodity.

Of great value to a woman's future. Though there had been females who'd surrendered their innocence outside of marriage for a multitude of reasons, he'd never known a woman to go to such lengths to purposely discard it.

"Foolishly, I thought it was the perfect plan," she continued. "No one knew of my presence at the masquerade, and with a mask, I maintained my anonymity."

"Except I removed your mask in bed," he reminded her.

"It didn't matter. You didn't know me. You never asked my name. And I purposely didn't ask for yours, so that it couldn't be coerced from me by my father later on. I didn't want to involve you in my situation any more than I had to."

Adrien arched a brow. "You didn't know who I was? You didn't know anything about me when you stole into my room?"

She gave a mirthless laugh. "Only that you were from Vienna."

"Vienna?"

She shook her head. "It's what my maid told me—obviously in error. A foreigner was the perfect choice. I wasn't supposed to ever see you again. Clearly, with my many mistakes, it was a plan doomed to fail. My greatest error was in believing that in the end my father would open his eyes and ultimately choose his daughter's happiness over his own wants."

Her words stabbed into Adrien, her remarks resonating inside him.

A single tear slipped down her cheek. Impatiently, she swiped it away. "I was wrong about the depth of my father's affection. I guess I'd hoped he actually cared."

Adrien felt as though he'd stumbled upon a kindred spirit. And that was the last thing he thought he'd discover about her.

He turned away and raked a hand through his hair, tamping down the soft sentiment welling up inside him. "Why the aphrodisiac?" he asked, staring at the shadows and light on the wall above the torchère.

"How did you know it had been added to the wine?"

Adrien turned back around. "I found a powdery substance at

the bottom of my goblet the next morning. Given the heated intensity of our encounter, it wasn't difficult to guess what the powder was." He crossed his arms. "You still haven't answered my question: why the aphrodisiac?"

"I have no idea how to seduce a man. The aphrodisiac ensured success. I couldn't very well approach you and say, 'Excuse me, would you care to bed me?' What if you had refused?"

Dieu. Could she really have no idea how desirable she was? "Catherine, had you made that proposition to every man in that room, you'd have had unanimous acceptance of your offer. No man would have refused you."

A pretty blush colored her cheeks, obviously unaccustomed to compliments about her appeal.

"Didn't your husband ever tell you how beautiful you are?" From the sounds of it, Villecourt had been a colossal ass, but surely in the throes of passion he'd stated the obvious, no? The vision she made naked in Adrien's bed still haunted him to this day.

"No. Never. He indicated . . . quite the opposite, in fact." She lifted her chin a notch. "He had no desire for me, in or out of the boudoir." Those statements were weighted with hurt and suffering and Adrien couldn't help but admire her bravado. No doubt Villecourt had had a favorite mistress—thus the reason for his disinterest.

"You said he'd found different ways to torment you. Do those ways relate to the scandal you've mentioned?"

Reluctantly, she nodded.

"What did he do, Catherine?" He had no idea why the hell he was asking questions about her marriage. Why did any of it matter?

"He"—she clasped and unclasped her hands—"gleefully made us the talk of every salon in Paris. It was not easy to live in the city as he carried on with his . . . lovers. After the first few months of our marriage, he made no attempt to hide them at all."

This was puzzling. "Who was he bedding? What made them so noteworthy?"

She let out a sharp exasperated breath, her expression a mixture of agony and anger. "If you must know every sordid detail of my marriage, I shall tell you from beginning to end, although I don't understand why Villecourt should interest you. My late husband only came to my bed twice and under duress because of pressure from his family to procure an heir. Each distasteful time he told me he found me repulsive. It wasn't until I walked in on him having sex with one of the servants that I learned the true reason for his disgust. My husband didn't desire me because I wasn't . . ."

"What?"

"A . . . man."

Now there was an answer Adrien hadn't expected, though he should have. What other reason could there be for a man to find this ravishing woman undesirable?

She approached him. "You asked who he was bedding. He was bedding most of our male staff as well as men of higher rank. His favorite was the Baron de Nogaret. He became quite open about his sexual preferences and even tried to blame me for them. His involvement in a lovers' triangle—Nogaret the object of interest for Villecourt and the Comte de Ragon—led to his demise. He died in a duel over his favorite male paramour." She opened her arms. "There. Now you know the horrid truth. All of it. Because of him, I've endured pitying looks, mortifying whispers." She held up a dainty finger an inch from the end of his nose. "I want you to know he didn't break me. He tried. But I remained strong, despite his vicious tongue, the humiliating gossip, the financial ruin. I don't want anyone's pity—"

Adrien pressed his fingers to her lips, silencing her. He'd lost all desire to use her as a pawn. He didn't have the stomach to put her through more scandal. He'd find another way, another opportunity to drive his point home to his sire. "I think you are strong and brave." He removed his hand from her soft lips.

Those were words he'd never uttered to a woman before.

"Oh." Catherine's eyes softened. "Thank you . . . I truly meant it when I said I was sorry. I regret the trickery. But not our night." He didn't know why but her statement pleased him immensely. "If I had it to do again, I would proposition you instead of . . . doing what I did to your wine. If you will permit me, I have a proposition to make to you now."

"Oh?"

She bit her delectable bottom lip, something he was dying to do. "For your silence about the event that occurred five years ago, I will . . . I would be . . . your mistress for the next five days."

His semihard cock turned stone stiff at the inflaming offer. "For five days?"

"Yes, that's when Philbert will arrive." She glanced down and noticed the blatant bulge of his erection. When she looked up, she was smiling, clearly feeling confident of his answer. "What say you?"

Adrien tilted his head to the side. "For my silence you're willing to do this?"

"Yes. I am yours for five days." She clasped her hands behind her back—a purposeful pose that caused her bodice to gape open, giving him a better view of her tempting tits.

"Interesting . . . a day for every year since the masquerade." A day for every year he'd fantasized about her. Days and nights to indulge in each and every fantasy.

"Yes." She was still smiling.

He stepped closer, their bodies all but touching, and slipped his fingers under her chin. "Your proposition is difficult to refuse."

She maintained his regard, her golden eyes darkening with desire. "Is it now?"

He brushed his lips against her warm mouth. "Hmmm . . . it is."

"And"—she swallowed—"what is your answer . . . ?"

He trailed his mouth along her jaw to her ear. "My answer is . . ." he murmured and nipped at her earlobe, making her gasp. "No."

CHAPTER SEVEN

Catherine's mouth fell agape. She clamped it shut the moment she realized Adrien was stalking toward the door.

"Wait!" she called out.

To her relief, he stopped abruptly and turned around.

Flustered and suddenly afraid, she marched up to him. "Why not?" She gestured toward the bulge in his breeches. "You are clearly interested."

"I don't want a woman who is intent on playing a martyr in bed. I told you, I have no intention of telling the King or anyone about what happened between us. I came here for answers. You supplied them. The matter is done. Laid to rest. So, if you want sex, Catherine, say so. If you'd like to indulge in carnal pleasures with me for the next few days, be honest about it. I'll not entertain any more deceptions or denials from you. Speak to me of desire and I am interested. Speak to me of this ridiculous martyrdom, and I will direct my 'interest' elsewhere."

"All right! Yes, I desire you," she blurted out.

He crossed his arms. "Go on."

He wasn't going to make this easy, was he? "I have always desired you. From the moment I saw you across the Grand Salon at the masquerade that night, I . . . craved you. You stirred a hunger in me. I am famished for more. I've yearned for you countless nights. I want you to be my lover. I want to revel in all the carnal delights you can bestow. I want to know what I missed in my marriage bed and what I will miss in the next. Is that honest enough for you?"

His sinfully tempting mouth lifted in a smile. "It is an excellent start." He removed his justacorps and tossed the knee-length coat carelessly to the floor. "Here are the conditions for our interlude of bliss—"

"Conditions?"

He tilted her chin up with his strong warm fingers. "My conditions are as follows: You will give me carte blanche in bed. You will let me have you as often as I want, any way I choose, without reservation or inhibitions getting in the way. Agreed?"

A thrill rippled down her spine. "Agreed."

Smiling, he pulled her up against his large sculpted body. "Good. This is a perfect time to begin, wouldn't you say?"

She flattened her palms on his chest. "Wait."

"Wait?"

"I haven't given you *my* conditions."

"*Your* conditions?" He asked the question as though no one had ever given him any.

"Yes. They are as follows: You will give me carte blanche in bed. You will let me have you as often as I want, any way I choose, without reservation or inhibitions getting in the way."

He burst into laughter. "Ah, Catherine, you are a delight. I am very much looking forward to the next few days, my spirited lady. It seems we are in accord." He lowered his head for a kiss.

She pressed her fingers against his lips, arresting his descent. "I'm not through. In addition, you will be all mine. For five days, there will be no other woman. Just me."

The astounded look on his handsome face was darling. Clearly, no one had ever made that request of him.

Catherine stepped back. "Well? What say you to that?"

The corner of his mouth jerked as he fought back his amusement. "I say you're about to obtain an unprecedented promise from me. I agree to your wish of exclusivity." He pulled her back into his arms. His delicious erection, so solid and thick, pressed enticingly against her belly. "Anything else? Or can we begin?"

"One last thing."

His head fell back with a groan. "What is it, *ma belle*? Be quick so that we can move on to more pleasurable pursuits."

"I wish the utmost discretion. No one is to know about our arrangement. The last thing I want is to give gossipmongers more to talk about. Or to cause Philbert the sort of pain and embarrassment Villecourt caused me."

Adrien's jaw tightened, his expression difficult to discern. Then he brushed his knuckles along her cheek. "No one will know," he softly pledged. Taking her hand, he pressed his warm lips to her palm. Sensations tingled up her arm. "Come." His voice, low and husky, reverberated down to her sex.

He led her out of the antechamber into the bedchamber. Thinking about what he would do to her, what she wanted him to do to her, raced her pulse. She'd given him carte blanche. She couldn't explain it, this wanton she became around him. But she didn't dwell on it. Not when she was on fire for him.

Adrien was all hers for the next five days. She was going to relish every moment of it.

Stopping at the foot of the bed, he released her hand. His gaze perused her body. With her bodice open, she felt cool air against her heated skin, but it did nothing to diminish the fever he inspired. Anticipation made her tremble. The ache between her legs was fierce. If he didn't touch her soon, she'd die.

Impatient, Catherine pulled off the pearl necklace she'd borrowed from Suzanne and dropped it on the bed. Grabbing his shirt, she crushed her lips against his and thrust her tongue into his mouth. His taste was intoxicating. Her kiss was ravenous, stroking and sucking his tongue. Delirious with need, she couldn't get enough.

Cradling her face between his palms, he slanted his mouth over hers and gave her a slower, more languorous kiss.

Her frustration squeaked out her throat. Determined to quicken the pace, she reached down and grabbed hold of the ties on his breeches, desperate to free him of his clothing, to touch his skin once more, but her hands shook and her fingers fumbled.

He stilled her frantic hands. "I like your enthusiasm," he murmured against her mouth. "But there's no need to rush. We're going to savor every sensation. Slow down. I promise, it will be just as good."

Slow down? Was he mad? She was about to expire on the spot with lust. "I'd like to 'savor every sensation' quickly."

He let out a chuckle and shook his head. "Be patient."

His answer was exasperating, but at least he was untying his breeches. Riveted on his deft fingers, she doubted she'd notice if the room caught on fire.

At last, he freed his shirt from his breeches and removed it, tossing it to the floor.

Her eyes feasted on his strong shoulders. His chiseled chest. And—her gaze moved down his body—the impressive cock straining out of his breeches, the sight weakening her knees, making the nub between her legs throb.

The corner of his mouth rose as he clasped her wrist and brought her hand to his shaft. She eagerly curled her fingers around him. His skin was warm, velvety, yet he was thick and solid. "Is this what you need, Catherine?"

Oh, God. "Yes."

"How long has it been since a man made you come the way I made you come today?"

He wanted to talk? *Now?*

"Tell me . . ." he urged softly. With his hold on her wrist, Adrien was keeping her from stroking him the way she yearned to.

She licked her dry lips. "Five years, two months, and one week. The night of the masquerade . . . with *you.*"

His green eyes darkened. "*Jésus-Christ.* Everything you do, everything you say, makes me want to fuck you."

Joy and excitement fluttered in her belly. "Then take me."

He dipped his head and kissed the sensitive spot below her ear. "I will. I'll ride you all night long. You'd like that, wouldn't you?" He stroked her hand down the length of his erection and then back up. Her sex clenched. "Answer me, Catherine. Tell me you want my cock inside you all night long." Adrien trailed his mouth along her neck and released her hand, leaving her free to stroke him on her own.

"Yes. I want your . . . cock inside me. I want you to take me again and again until we're sated." She'd never spoken like this in her life. Never uttered such brazen statements. Never voiced her wants. Not for many years now. They'd always been ignored. Except by him. He'd been the only one who'd ever given her what she wanted. And true bliss.

"As you wish," he whispered in her ear; she heard the smile in his voice. Slipping his hand inside her opened bodice, he rolled her hardened nipple between his fingers, his delicious torment sending wave after wave of sharp pleasure streaking from the tip of her breast down to her heated core. Her sex ached to be filled. Enveloped by scintillating sensations, she closed her eyes. Suddenly, her clothing was too hot, her skin too warm. The urges too powerful, thundering in her blood.

"Now . . . Adrien." She panted. "I need . . ."

"I know what you need, beautiful Catherine . . ." He stripped away her clothing, discarding each article onto the floor. She didn't care what he did with her clothes, though she had precious few good things left. She wanted her garments off. His garments off. His skin against her skin. She wanted him inside her and the divine friction their bodies created.

She tried to help with the removal of her clothing, but ceased when she realized she was only impeding his progress. Instead, she used the moments to gaze at his beautiful face, desire and determination etched thereon.

As soon as her *caleçons* and chemise hit the floor, he tossed her onto the bed. She landed on the mattress with a surprised gasp and a small bounce. She rose onto her elbows, quivering from the inside out. Standing at the foot of the bed, Adrien discarded the remainder of his clothing.

"Open your legs for me," he growled in all his naked glory.

Her heart missed a beat. A heady rush of excitement swamped her. Slowly, she parted her thighs, her face feeling red-hot. One at a time, he sank his knees into the mattress between her legs.

"Bend your knees, Catherine. Let me look at all of you." He ran his warm palms over her trembling thighs.

Biting her lip, her heart wildly pounding, she obliged, leaving herself completely open to his view. His features softened, and he stroked his fingers along her slick flesh. A moan slipped past her lips. His touch was light and so deliciously decadent.

"You're very beautiful . . . Everywhere."

His words swirled around her heart, when she knew she shouldn't let them.

"I haven't forgotten a single detail about you," he said.

Neither had she, though not from lack of trying. No amount of wishing had made her unlearn what she'd discovered in his arms.

"You're wet. Ripe for the taking," he said with a wicked smile on his face. He lowered himself on top of her. His mouth was only inches from hers, their breaths, ragged and rapid, mingling together. The press of his body was sublime. Despite the urgency coursing through her veins, she tenderly brushed his dark hair from his brow and gently cradled his cheeks between her palms.

He grasped her wrists and lowered them to the bed. "Catherine, this is about sex. Mutual pleasure. Nothing more."

She wasn't going to allow herself to forget that. "Yes, I know." She thought she heard something in his voice, or perhaps it was the way in which he spoke his words, as though he was trying to convince not only her, but himself as well. She instantly dismissed the notion as absurd.

"This is definitely about sex," she said with a saucy smile. She played with fire. A novice at recreational fornication, she could be burned, but what woman could resist the allure of Adrien d'Aspe? He could have anyone, and yet, "You want me."

He arched a brow. "You want my cock," he countered.

"You want to give it to me."

A chuckle rumbled in his chest. "On that point I'll cede." He stroked his hard length along the slick folds of her sex, grazing the head of his shaft over her clitoris and back down, muffling her whimper with a hungry kiss.

He released her wrists. She had her arms around him in an instant, returning his kiss with equal intensity.

He tore his mouth from hers. "To hell with this prolongation. It will be as you want—fast and hard." Rolling off, he flipped her onto her stomach.

Startled by the suddenness of his actions, she looked over her shoulder at him. "Adrien . . ."

His face contorted by desire, he snaked an arm under her hips and lifted her derrière in the air. Her fever spiked. "I'm going to give you what you want. What I want. What we're here for."

Her warm cheek against the cool sheets, she quaked with anticipation, her legs wobbly and weak, desperate for his possession.

He dug his fingers into her hips and wedged the head of his sex at her entrance. She choked back a sob. Instead of driving into her as she longed, he slowly slid his broad shaft inside her, stretching and filling her an inch at a time, working his way deeper and deeper.

He groaned. "You have the tightest, sweetest cunt."

She shut her eyes and gripped the sheets, unable to find her voice, to protest against his unhurried penetration. The moment he'd finally fed her his whole length, her legs gave out. She collapsed to the bed, his body following hers down.

He reared then and used his strength and weight to drive his cock back into her, hard and deep. She cried out, enraptured. Trapped beneath him, his large form pressing her into the mattress, she took each powerful thrust, unable to move, the friction inflaming her further.

"This is how you want it, isn't it, Catherine?" he said near her ear between harsh breaths.

"Yes!" Her body was awash with sensations, her every nerve

ending vibrating with life. She clenched her inner muscles. He let out a sharp groan. Realizing there was a way to affect him in this position after all, she clutched and released around his thick thrusting shaft. He grunted with each plunge as she milked him toward his climax.

Without breaking his rhythm, he shoved his hand under her hips and found the pulsing bud between her legs. He fingered her with devastating finesse. She whimpered, the beginnings of her orgasm suddenly barreling down on her.

"Adrien . . . I'm… going to . . ."

"Come for me . . . Do it!" He pinched her clit.

Catherine screamed into the mattress, her release shaking her to the core. Being with this man was the greatest joy she'd ever known.

Chapter Eight

Catherine awoke to the sound of a steady heartbeat beneath her ear and two strong arms around her. Her cheek resting on a very masculine, solid chest, she peeked up to see Adrien fast asleep. Carefully, she rose onto her elbow and allowed herself the simple pleasure of gazing at him. His cheekbones, straight nose, jaw and kissable mouth were etched forever in her mind. It was incredible, really. She'd envisioned this very visage for years and here he was. In the flesh. In her arms. Not just a fantasy come to life, but a dream come true.

Lightly, she caressed his cheek. He stirred in his sleep.

She couldn't hold back her smile.

The slight tenderness between her legs was a pleasing reminder of their glorious night. Unaccustomed to sexual excess, she should have been exhausted, but she wasn't. Not in the least. Last eve had been a night of incomparable bliss—so similar to their interlude five years ago when she'd awoken with the same rare sense of happiness that had nothing to do with the success of her ill fated plan. And everything to do with him.

She didn't have to sneak away this time.

This time they'd enjoyed a compatibility that was not just physical. Between rapturous diversions, they'd laughed. Teased. Talked. Though she understood the boundaries of their relationship, she yearned to know more about this man. She sensed a profound unrest in him that resonated in her.

Catherine was about to snuggle back down beneath the bedding when a thought occurred to her.

Odette.

She glanced at the window. The sun shone brightly. It was well past dawn. Her loyal maid would arrive at any moment. Though she loved the woman dearly, eccentric in her ways, one never could predict Odette's behavior. It was best to avoid embarrassment all around and not have poor Odette stumble upon Adrien in her bed.

Reluctantly, Catherine eased herself from Adrien's arms.

Scooping up her chemise, she threw it on, quietly dashed from the bedchamber, softly closing the door behind her. She got three steps into the antechamber when she heard a woman's scream.

Catherine closed her eyes. *Too late.*

Wrenching open the door, she ran back into the other room.

Odette stood beside the bed with her hands covering her eyes. Adrien was sitting up, a murderous look directed at her maid, clearly irked by her presence and the way she'd startled him awake.

Why couldn't the woman have used the door in the antechamber, as was her practice, rather than the bedchamber door?

"Odette," Catherine said.

Upon hearing her name, her maid dropped her hands. Her gaze shot to Catherine. "I—I'm sorry, madame. I—I had no idea you had . . . company." She glanced at Adrien, let out a squeak, and slapped her palms over her eyes once again.

Adrien rolled his eyes and reclined into the pillows.

From Catherine's vantage point, he was a sight to behold. His dark hair was mussed, his sculpted chest was bare, and the bedding lay tantalizingly across his waist—the outline of his shaft visible to her hungry eyes.

This was a first. She, Catherine de Villecourt, had never had a man with such potent appeal in her bed.

Stop ogling. Collect yourself. Say something.

She formed a smile. "Good morning, Adrien."

The wicked gleam in his eyes made her knees weak. "Good morning, Catherine." Oh, the way he said her name. She felt a quickening in her belly.

"If you will excuse me, I'll return momentarily." She grasped Odette's arm. The older woman's hands were still affixed to her face.

He slipped his hands under his head. "Hurry back." A slight smile tilted the corner of his mouth. Those two seemingly innocuous words held such sinful promise.

"I will." She dragged Odette toward the door to the antechamber. Tossing a glance at her maid, she noticed Odette's head was slightly turned toward the bed and her fingers were separated, giving her left eye a clear view of Adrien.

"Odette," Catherine scolded in a firm whisper.

Odette's fingers immediately closed and her head snapped forward.

The moment they were behind closed doors, Odette removed her hands from her eyes and slapped them over her mouth just as a fit of giggles seized her.

Catherine placed her hands on her hips, ready to chastise her, but with her heart so light, she found herself fighting back a giant smile.

"Oh, madame, I'm sorry." Odette tried to sober up. "But it's just a delightful surprise . . ." Another giggle bubbled out of her. "Your handsome Marquis looks even better abed."

Catherine dropped her arms to her sides with a wistful sigh. "He does look very good, doesn't he?"

"Most definitely!" Odette's eyes widened. "And he is so big."

"Yes, he is a tall man."

"No, no, madame, I mean he is *large*." She held out her hands several inches apart and wiggled her brows.

Catherine blushed. "Odette, really now . . ."

"There is plenty there to delight a lady." Joviality erupted from her again. She covered her mouth once more to muffle it.

The last thing Catherine wanted to do was encourage Odette,

but a full smile tugged hard at the corners of Catherine's lips, despite herself. "There is much about him that would delight any woman," she responded. There was much about Adrien d'Aspe that delighted *her*. Sinful skills, looks, and charm aside, to her surprise, he was an avid reader. He enjoyed books. He enjoyed all of the same Latin and Spanish classics as she did. Moreover, he had compassion. The understanding he'd demonstrated when she'd confided the circumstances surrounding the masquerade moved her. The kindness and interest he'd shown in her paintings touched her.

Catherine knew she was on dangerous ground. These tender emotions she felt would only bring heartache if she didn't somehow quash them.

"I take it you've worked things out with Monsieur le Marquis, then?"

"Yes, we are in accord. In fact, for the next few days I need you to—"

"Say no more, madame. What happened just now will not be repeated. I'll be most discreet and circumspect. Now, go on. Enjoy your handsome Marquis." Odette rushed to the door leading to the hallway, then stopped and turned with a smile. "Madame, if I may say one last thing before I go?"

"Of course. What is it, Odette?"

"I'm so very happy to see you like this. If you could only see your face . . . It is aglow. And your eyes sparkle as they never have before."

*****

Three days later.

The scent of jasmine lingered on his skin as Adrien strolled back to his rooms with a smile. Memories of the last few hours making love to Catherine ran through his mind. He'd awoken her that morning by gently sucking that sweet little bud between her legs; the friction of his tongue and the pull of his mouth as he alternated licking and suckling her sensitive nub had sent her straight into a strong orgasm.

Each afternoon they'd sneaked back to her chambers. Each morning he left her rooms later than the day before.

The fact that he stayed the night—every night—was novel in itself. He found himself anxiously awaiting their next private moment. The next stirring kiss from her luscious mouth. His attraction to her went well beyond the physical. He simply liked being with her. Talking to her. Laughing with her. He couldn't remember a time when he'd enjoyed a woman's company more. They were compatible in every way.

Deliciously sensual, intelligent, beautiful and brave, she was a breath of fresh air in his world.

She was different from other women. Everything with her was different. He *wanted* to know more about her, know all her interests. Seeing the happy glow in her amber-colored eyes as she spoke of her painting and her favorite books pleased him more than he could ever admit. This level of intimacy and connection was new to him, and he didn't know why or how she'd inspired it.

He refused to dwell on his unprecedented actions or try to decipher the meaning behind them. They had two days and nights left. He wanted to revel in every moment with her. Stay in the present and not consider the future when she left.

Thinking about Catherine back in his arms in a few short hours quickened his heart. His smile grew. He had a plan for this afternoon he knew would delight her.

Reaching the door to his chambers, he opened the latch and entered his rooms. Charlotte was seated near the window. She rose as he closed the door.

"What are you doing here, Charlotte? You have your own private apartments."

A smile formed on her face. "Your bed hasn't been slept in."

"So?"

"So, you've been entertaining Catherine de Villecourt."

He sighed, resentful that his genial mood was about to be threatened. "Charlotte . . ." he began and tossed his justacorps onto a nearby chair.

"You're doing admirably! The plan is working beautifully."

Adrien took in a deep breath and let it out slowly, grasping for patience. "I am not doing 'admirably.' There is no plan. I'm not going to be part of your scheme, Charlotte."

"Ah, but you are." She walked up to him and placed her hand on his arm. "I've seen the way she looks at you in the gardens, at each meal, when she thinks no one is observing her. She's quite smitten."

"Catherine is not the problem. Whether she marries Baillet or not, it won't change your situation."

"It will! Philbert wouldn't be so distracted . . . Things between us will be as they were before." Her eyes glistened with tears. "I already lost Jean-Paul. His death almost killed me. I cannot lose Philbert, too."

"Charlotte, you are looking for someone to blame for Baillet's disinterest, but the reality is—"

"Stop!" She pressed a trembling hand against his chest. "I don't want to hear any more. Philbert still loves me. He does! You'll not convince me otherwise. You don't know him as I do."

"Charlotte, if he loved you, no woman could distract him, *ma chère*. Don't you see that?"

"Wh-Why are you being so cruel?" Tears spilled down her cheeks. "Why do you want to hurt me? Just because you're not happy, you don't want me to be happy." She ran to the door, audibly sobbing.

"Charlotte, wait! That's not it. I want your happiness."

Grabbing the door latch, she threw him a vicious glare. "I hate you, Adrien," she cried. "*I hate you.*" She ran from the room as if he were Lucifer himself.

Adrien remained frozen, the air around him suddenly heavy and cold.

Sinking into a chair, he rested his elbows on his thighs and shook his head. *Merde*, how had things come full circle? How many times had he heard one of his uncles have the very same conversation with his mother? How many times had his mother reacted just as Charlotte had? There was no point chasing after Charlotte. She'd be inconsolable for hours yet.

Tossing his head back, he closed his eyes and took in a fortifying breath. This was what happened when one blurred the lines between sex and love. A mistake he'd never make. The soft sentiments he was feeling for Catherine had to be reined in. Kept in check.

She was his *temporary* mistress.

In two days she'd be gone. In two days he would have satiated himself. He had two more days in which to purge her from his blood and mind. He couldn't, wouldn't, crave her or think of her after that.

With renewed determination, he stalked out of his rooms intent on making afternoon arrangements with his lovely midnight temptress.

In his experience the only thing that cooled a carnal fever was sexual excess.

CHAPTER NINE

"A few steps further," Adrien said behind Catherine, his warm hands covering her eyes.

Trusting him implicitly, she moved forward, letting him guide her blindly.

"Perfect." He arrested her steps and pulled his hands away.

She opened her eyes and grinned, ridiculously happy over the sight before her.

In a clearing, beneath a large tree, in the forest that bordered Suzanne's grounds, a blanket had been spread, encircled by flower petals of white, yellow and lavender. A basket of food had been placed nearby.

A picnic.

It was lovely!

Catherine turned and wrapped her arms around his neck.

The gray skies overhead let out a grumble.

She ignored the distant thunder. This moment was too perfect. Keeping their encounters secret hadn't been easy. He'd gone to such touching lengths to make these preparations.

"You planned all this for me." It was a statement. She was incredulous.

"Of course." He was smiling. "You're pleased?"

She gazed at his beloved face. "I am. Thank you. No one has ever done anything like this for me before."

He pulled her tightly against him, his erection pressing

against her. Arousal flared low in her belly. "Well, then, I am honored to be the first."

Oh, he was her first in so many ways. Her first lover. The only man to inspire her affections. She'd tried to fight her feelings with all she possessed, telling herself the joys he brought her were only physical. That she wasn't in love with him.

All unconvincing lies.

In truth, he'd slipped inside her heart—years ago. The times she'd spent with him were the happiest she'd ever known. But time was running out.

Glancing up at the sky, she was dismayed by the threat of rain in the darkened clouds. The day had started out sunny, but the sky became angrier as the hours passed.

"Forget the weather," he said. "We'll not allow anything to ruin our picnic." He gently brushed an errant tress from her cheek. "Now, where were we . . . Ah yes, you were voicing words of appreciation for my efforts." He gave her one of his disarming smiles. "I am open to any and all expressions of gratitude, you know."

She laughed. "Are you now?" The cheeky devil oozed charm.

"I am," he assured. "However, I am happy to provide nourishment first." He nodded toward the picnic basket.

"That's excellent. I'm starved . . . *for you*." She caressed the side of his face.

Hunger flickered in his eyes. He leaned in for a kiss, sliding his tongue past her lips. Waves of pleasure flooded her body at his possession. His kiss was heated, yet unhurried and tender, resonating inside her heart.

Raindrops hit her shoulders, despite the leafy canopy overhead. She didn't care, refusing to break contact with his mouth. She wanted more. Of him. How was she going to live without him again? He made her long for the things she used to dream about. Romantic notions of loving and being loved.

The sky rumbled. More raindrops struck her heated skin.

Adrien broke the kiss and swore at the inclement weather brewing in the clouds, its quick turn for the worse dampening their plans.

She reached for the ties on his breeches and opened them with practiced haste. "We'll not allow anything to ruin our picnic." She repeated his words.

He frowned. "It's raining, *ma belle.*"

"It doesn't matter." She pulled his shirt out from his breeches. "Take this off."

He gave her one of his heart-fluttering smiles and removed his shirt, tossing it onto the blanket. His thick, hard cock strained out of his breeches.

A steady drizzle now fell from the sky. She watched with heated fascination as water droplets hit his chest, and rolled down his skin, and dripped off his stiff sex.

Desire swamped her senses. She had to touch him. Curling her fingers around his shaft, she stroked him, moving her hand languidly up and down his length.

He groaned. His mouth was on hers in an instant, his skilled fingers pulling and loosening and opening the front of her gown, exposing her to her waist.

Cool rain against her warm breasts was startling. Exhilarating. His hot mouth latched onto her breast. He sucked greedily. Each perfect pull of his mouth dragged a moan up her throat and made her sex wetter. She arched to him, her fingers tangling in his damp hair. He turned to her other breast and feasted on it with equal finesse. Suckling. Licking. Gently biting. Her legs almost gave way.

The moment his mouth returned to hers, she kissed him voraciously, trailing her mouth along his jaw, down his neck, his chest. His wet skin was delicious. But it wasn't enough. After a night of oral pleasures—not to mention the morning, too—she had to taste him again, hungry to have him in her mouth. Only two days left to create memories she'd cherish for a lifetime. Then he'd be gone for good. She pushed back the sadness and regret and lowered herself to her knees.

His eyes narrowed, knowing exactly what she was about. She looked up at him, rain on her face. His dark hair wet, he fixed his green eyes on her. Holding his gaze, she gripped the base of his erection and brushed her lips across the sensitive tip. His breath hitched. Reveling in his heated response, she swirled her tongue around the head of his penis.

"Catherine," he rasped, his fingers gripping her head.

Impatient, she plunged him deep into her mouth. A throaty growl erupted out of him, his hips jerking slightly.

"Dieu . . ." Adrien had to close his eyes, his head falling back. If the feel of her sucking his cock weren't enough, the sight of her submissively on her knees pleasuring him was too much. "I love your mouth," he groaned. It took everything he had not to grab her hair and thrust like a madman. Instead, he let her dictate the pace.

His ragged breaths mingled with the sounds of rain. The cool raindrops teeming over his bare chest and arms were a magnificent contrast to the heat of her mouth. She drew him in and dragged him out, tender, yet ravenous—so uniquely Catherine. She had him on fire, as always.

Every fiber of his being was acutely aware not only of the sensations inundating him, but of the very woman inspiring them. He was going to come. Hard. Soon. But not this way. Not this time.

Opening his eyes, their gazes locked. She slid him out of her mouth and licked off the dab of pre-come that dripped from his tip. Strands of her auburn hair were plastered to her shoulders and wet breasts. Gently removing her hand from his cock, Adrien lowered himself to his knees, the blanket wet, and cupped her face.

She furrowed her delicate brow. "Have I done something incorrectly?"

"No, you were perfect." She was, in every way that mattered. Everything a man could want and more.

And he wanted her—too much.

Threading his fingers through her wet hair, he ran his tongue along her bottom lip before giving her a long languorous kiss. A shiver of delight quivered through her.

"I want to make love to you." He sat down on the blanket, not caring that it was soaked. "Come here." His voice was rough with need.

The sweetest smile graced her lips.

A few easy movements and his auburn beauty was straddling him. She slipped her arms around him. Her breaths were sharp and shallow, much like his own. A surge of emotions he couldn't quell crested over him.

Jésus-Christ, he simply had to break this infatuation. What if he couldn't? What if years from now he still felt this constricting ache in his chest?

Adrien shoved away the doubts, and her gown, bunching the material around her waist. He then gripped her hips, intent on refocusing on the carnal pleasures at hand.

"I am all yours," she said softly, placing her hands on his wet shoulders.

Her words unbalanced him.

She was *not* all his, he quickly reminded himself. Even if he wished it at the moment. In time the feeling would pass. He wasn't going to do anything to hold on to her or deviate from old patterns and familiar ways.

She rose up and brought her slick opening down onto the head of his cock, the enticing heat beckoning and beguiling. Her pink nipples, at mouth level, dripped with raindrops.

Adrien leaned in and licked the water droplets off each sensitive tip.

She moaned and then suddenly bore down onto his erection. Clutching her hips, he halted her descent. "Too fast. Take it slowly." Adrien eased her onto his cock, her moist heat engulfing him an inch at a time.

She squirmed, frustrated by his slow progress.

"Don't fight me. Just enjoy it." He was going to squeeze out every ounce of pleasure he could from the encounters they had left, hoping it would be enough to silence the maddening turmoil whirling inside him.

The head of his shaft butted against her womb. He gasped.

She whimpered.

Buried to the hilt, his cock throbbed inside her snug sheath. She encircled him with her legs. Adrien closed his eyes and held her still. Enveloped by her, he basked in the moment.

Endearingly impatient, it wasn't long before she was rocking her hips, fanning the fire, making his heart pound. She clenched her inner muscles around his cock. A groan shot up his throat.

Kissing his face, mouth, neck, she told him how much she wanted him, needed him, needed what he could give her. Adrien's control snapped. In an instant, he had her on her back, giving her perfect sex deep steady stokes, using his body to shield her from the rain. Holding her gaze, he increased the tempo and force of his thrusts with each downward plunge.

Desire shone in her golden eyes. Yearning was etched on her lovely face.

"You're so very beautiful," he murmured.

Her hands moved tenderly down his back, despite her feverish state. "So are you."

Her artlessness during sex was adorable.

The tension coiling tighter and tighter, they were racing toward a shattering release. Shaking with effort, he held his back, the need to let go and discharge his aching cock immense.

She sucked in a sharp breath, squeezed her eyes shut, and arched hard against him. "Adrien," she cried. He braced himself. Her orgasm shuddered through her, tearing a scream from her throat.

Fisting the blanket on either side of her head, Adrien thrust fiercely, glorious spasms rippling along his length. His climax triggered, his release shot down his cock with such volatile force, he barely pulled out in time. Collapsing on top of her, he pressed his forehead to hers and groaned long and hard as he drained his prick onto the blanket with mind-melting intensity.

Spent, trembling, they held each other, the rain drizzling onto his back, their breathing slowly calming.

This was bliss. How fortunate was he to be given this taste of Heaven.

Another roll of thunder sounded in the sky.

*****

Catherine and Adrien stopped outside the servants' entrance to the château. Catherine sighed as he gave her a deep stirring kiss. They were drenched, their clothing ruined, and neither of them cared. They'd walked back in the heavy rain, hand in hand, occasionally stopping for kisses and caresses.

"I'm sorry our picnic was spoiled," he murmured. "The food was ruined."

"I don't think the picnic was spoiled at all. I enjoyed every moment."

A smile formed on his lips. "So did I."

She cocked her head to one side. "I'm sure the rain has nothing to do with the fact that you're cursed," she teased.

His brows shot up. "Oh, Lord. Don't tell me you've heard about that. What version of that foolish tale was recounted? The one with magical fairies at my christening?"

She laughed. "I missed that version."

"There is no curse," he assured. "I don't get along with my father. Plain and simple. He doesn't approve of the way I live my life. He thinks me too reckless."

"And are you?"

He brushed his mouth against hers. "I'm just reckless enough." He kissed her again, a slow inflaming kiss that warmed her blood, heating her from the inside out.

Thunder boomed. She jumped.

Adrien looked up at the sky, rain drizzling on his face. "We'd best get inside." He took her hand. "There will be more of the same on your dry bed," he wickedly promised.

The moment they stepped into the kitchens, Odette swooped in on them. "Madame!" Concern etched on her face, she wrung her hands.

Catherine tensed. "What is it, Odette?"

The older woman looked around to ensure none of the servants in the kitchen were listening.

"It's the Comte de Baillet," she whispered. "He's here."

Her words hit Catherine like a blow to the belly.

"He's arrived? *Early?*" Adrien asked the questions she couldn't force up her throat.

"Yes, monsieur. Early." Odette looked at Catherine. "He's asking for you. He's eager to see you."

Adrien tightened his hold of Catherine's hand. "It's too soon. He's not supposed to be here now," he growled.

Tears burned in her eyes. Catherine turned to him, overcome by a sense of cold grief and sadness. "I know," she managed to say without collapsing into complete discomposure. Their time together was over. She'd have to leave. Every fiber in her being screamed, "No!"

"Madame, we must get you upstairs, bathed, and changed into some dry clothes. I told Monsieur le Comte that you were taking a nap. He'll expect you up soon."

Catherine gazed at Adrien's cherished face, a lump welling in her throat.

He cupped her cheek. "I'll see you later," he stated firmly and kissed her trembling mouth.

"Come, madame." Odette pulled at her hand. "You must hurry."

Her chest tight, her heart constricted, she let Odette lead her away.

Time was up. There'd be no later.

CHAPTER TEN

In the *Salle de Buffet*, flanked by his uncles, Adrien held his goblet in a white-knuckle grip. He hadn't touched any of his meal. At the opposite end of the long table Catherine sat with Baillet and Suzanne. The dimwitted Madame de Noisette and Madame de Bussy were nearby enraptured by Baillet's tales of his recent visit to Versailles.

Adrien was drowning in emotions he'd forbidden himself to feel. Choking on his own misery.

Catherine was leaving.

Too damned soon.

Damn Baillet and his early arrival. Adrien felt cheated and furious at the situation. And at himself, for allowing feelings to foster.

"Perhaps we should check on Charlotte?" Paul suggested. "She was quite overwrought after her visit with Baillet this afternoon."

Charles shook his head. "Leave her be. She sleeps, the seasoned wine thankfully aiding in that regard."

Wine seasoned with the juice from unripe poppies. A concoction Adrien's mother had often consumed, especially after visits from his father. Today Baillet advised Charlotte that he wasn't interested in her company any longer—of course, only *after* a final fuck.

Charlotte was devastated.

News of his sister's distress only added fuel to Adrien's ire.

Eyes narrowed, Adrien drained his goblet as he watched Baillet dip his head toward Catherine in conversation, blocking her from his view. Seeing his proximity to her was torture. The thought of Baillet claiming his conjugal rights was all consuming.

"I should call him out," Adrien snarled. A murderous rage burbled in his blood.

"For what?" Robert asked. "For dismissing his mistress? Does a man not have the right to end an affair when he wants, Adrien? Let it alone. Dueling Baillet over something like this would definitely set off the King."

His father could go to hell, for all he cared.

"Your contempt for Baillet isn't simply over Charlotte," Paul said. "The lovely Catherine de Villecourt plays a part, no?"

Just then Baillet sat back and covered Catherine's hand with his.

The possessive gesture was a stinging sight.

Adrien looked away. "I need to speak to her." He rose, his chair dragging across the wooden floor.

Charles's eyes widened. "Now?"

"Yes. Now. This minute." *Merde*, the anguish was unbearable. "Have Suzanne escort her to the library—alone. Keep Baillet busy in the meantime. Perhaps expressing some dismay over his treatment of Charlotte, regardless of his 'rights,' would not only be warranted, but will also keep him occupied."

*****

Adrien paced in the library, his heart beating in hard rapid thumps. He was on unfamiliar ground. For the first time in his adult life, a woman had slipped past his defenses. The fact that an affair was dwindling down was not new—only the reactions he was having.

The door opened.

He stopped dead in his tracks as Catherine stepped inside and Suzanne, who'd been with her, promptly and quietly left, closing the door without a word.

His eyes devoured the sight of her. His midnight temptress. An angel. In but a simple yellow gown, her hair up with long auburn ringlets teasing her shoulders, she was ravishing.

Unshed tears glistened in her eyes, her sorrowful expression stabbing into him.

The next thing he knew, he'd crossed the distance between them and was holding her in his arms. "Catherine . . ." he breathed, pressing his cheek against her soft hair.

She trembled. So did he.

Adrien looked down at her upturned face and swooped in for a hungry kiss, needing her mouth with shocking desperation.

She broke the kiss sooner than he wanted. "Adrien . . . I'm leaving tomorrow."

His stomach clenched. "Why so soon? You are not getting married for another two weeks."

"He wishes to return to Baillet. I must go with him."

Don't go. Stay with me. Adrien swallowed down the words just in time. He hadn't uttered those words in years. Not since a life-altering day. He wouldn't beg. Or plead. Or lay himself emotionally bare that way. He'd never utter those words to anyone again.

"One last time." He caressed her cheek. "I need you one last time." He prayed for a miracle. For it to be enough to sate his need for her at last. Somehow, someway he had to silence what he was feeling. Her leaving was tearing him apart. "I'll come to your rooms—"

She shook her head and pulled free of his embrace. "I can't. Now that he is here—"

"He'll be in your bed tonight?" The question tumbled from Adrien's lips, uncensored.

"No. He'll not come to my bed until we're wedded. He has said as much. But . . ." A tear slipped down her cheek. She swiped it away. "Getting in that carriage tomorrow and leaving here, leaving . . . you . . . will be difficult enough as it is. If I spend the night in your arms . . . then tomorrow . . . the departure . . . will be unendurable torture."

Adrien turned away the moment he felt the mortifying sting of tears in his eyes. He was horrified by them. He was heartsick. The pain was so keen, like a blade slicing through him by slow excruciating degrees. This pain he knew. This was the pain he'd spent much of his life avoiding.

He spotted the brandy decanter on the ebony side table and stalked to it. Snatching up a goblet, he filled it with the amber liquid, his hands shaking. *Merde, collect yourself!*

By strength of will he'd master his emotions. He'd done so before. There was no reason to believe he couldn't do it again.

Adrien downed the fiery fluid, desperate for it to numb his insides. He heard her approach.

Catherine stopped beside him. He could see her from the corner of his eye, but couldn't bring himself to look at her. Instead, he stared at the goblet in his trembling hand as he fought to calm his sharp breaths.

She pulled the goblet from his grasp and placed it on the side table. "Adrien."

Against his better judgment, he met her gaze. Her lovely golden eyes were still filled with tears.

"I know this was supposed to be nothing more than an interlude of bliss," she said. "I understand the nature of our arrangement. I tried to hold to it, but couldn't separate heart and body. Sex and . . . love."

A lump welled in his throat. He wanted to tell her to stop. To say no more, but couldn't summon his voice.

"I love you, Adrien. What you have given me are memories I will treasure for the rest of my days."

He flinched. Women had uttered those words to him before. Why, when she spoke them, did he feel his soul tear? From her lips they had a stunning impact.

She cradled his face between her warm palms. Rising up onto the balls of her feet, she kissed him, her tears on her sweet lips.

The kiss was soft, poignant. It made him ache, heart, body and soul. His eyes closed of their own volition and he returned her kiss, unable to resist. Yet somehow, someway, though he yearned to touch her with every fiber of his being, he managed to keep his hands to himself, fearing that if he put his arms around her now, he'd never let go.

She broke the kiss. "Forgive me, but I wanted you to know how I felt. How much you mean to me. Thank you for what you've given me. I will think of you every day. And every night. You will be in my fondest dreams and most cherished thoughts." She stepped back.

He knew she was about to leave the room and walk out of his life.

Say something. Don't let her go. The voice rose from the empty chambers in his heart. But as Adrien stared back at her, he felt familiar walls rising up, steeling his resolve.

He cleared his throat before he croaked out, "I . . . wish you . . . much happiness."

With a woeful smile and a soft "thank you," she spun on her heel and walked out of the library, closing the door softly. With finality.

The silence roared in his ears.

In muted misery, Adrien stood alone for countless minutes, his chest heaving from the sheer exertion it took not to run to her.

Finally, he drew in a ragged breath and let it out slowly. He left the room on shaky limbs, forcing each foot forward, the decanter of brandy clutched firmly in one hand.

*****

Cold water splashed him in the face. Adrien sat bolt upright, startled out of slumber. A sharp pain ripped through his head.

Clutching his throbbing skull, he shot a string of expletives out of his mouth.

"Ah, good, you're awake," Charles said, holding an empty pitcher in his hand.

Adrien turned a dry raw eye to him. "*Merde*, what are you trying to do? Drown me?"

"I thought that is what you were doing to yourself—with

brandy."

He was in no mood for this. He'd spent the night and into the early morning hours imbibing, trying to obliterate visions of Catherine in Baillet's arms.

In Baillet's bed.

"Go away," Adrien snarled. Thanks to his uncle's antics, he and his bed were drenched.

"We need to talk. About women."

Adrien closed his eyes, willing the pounding in his brandy-soaked brain to stop. "You explained 'the mysteries of a woman's body' to me years ago, Uncle. I know everything I need to know about sex."

"Don't be so damned sarcastic. What I have to say to you is important. It involves your very happiness and future."

At the moment, the words "happiness" and "future" didn't seem to fit together.

The only thing greater than his headache was his longing for Catherine. Looking into the future, he had no idea when this torment would end, though he had every intention of quashing it, by any means necessary.

Charles stalked to the windows and threw open the curtains. Adrien squeezed his eyes shut against the blinding sunlight and cursed softly.

He heard his uncle pull a chair up beside his bed.

"I was much like you at your age," Charles said.

Jésus-Christ, he was serious about his desire to talk.

"Only I was better looking," Charles added.

Adrien pried open an eye and cast him a sidelong glance.

Seated, Charles chuckled and crossed his arms. "I see I have your attention. Good, then I'll continue. Like you, I too had my share of women. Still do, by the way."

"Uncle." Adrien opened both eyes as far as a squint, the light still too bright to tolerate. "I am well aware of your impressive sexual prowess. We are in accord on that point. What say you to ending this conversation?" All he wanted to do was sleep. Not think. Not talk. Or feel. Just sleep. Judging by the amount of sunlight in the room, the day had begun hours ago. He'd had very little repose.

"I say no. I also say, you're a fool. I know fools. I am one, too. Like you, I fell in love once."

Adrien was about to rebut when Charles held up a hand. "Say nothing. I saw your face last night when you looked at Catherine de Villecourt. You are in love with her. As in love as I was, *am still*, with her aunt, Elise—even these many years after her passing. I was about your age when I met her. She, like her niece, was beautiful." Charles's smile was woeful. "I used to think that love was as repugnant as an affliction. I'd seen it turn the brightest men into dimwits, while others writhed in agony when it slipped from their grasp. In short, love held no appeal for me." Charles unfolded his arms and briefly looked down at his hands. When he raised his gaze, Adrien saw his own anguish mirrored in his uncle's eyes. "I let her go, Adrien. I was madly, deeply in love and I let Elise go. I could have married her. We would have had joy-filled years together, perhaps even a child. Instead, I've had years of empty encounters and meaningless moments."

Adrien was speechless. This was a side of Charles he'd never known.

"Don't be as imbecilic as I, Adrien. Don't let Baillet have her. He doesn't deserve her. It isn't too late. She left a few hours ago. They'll be stopping at the town of Lagny for the night. Go to her. Tell her you love her."

The door burst open.

Robert and Paul entered, anxious expressions on their faces.

"Charlotte is gone." Paul held up a letter.

"What do you mean, gone?" Adrien rose from the bed, ignoring the stabbing pain that hit him between the eyes. His empty stomach roiled.

Robert snatched the letter from Paul's hand and brought it to Adrien. "When we went to check on her, we found this. She says she's going after Baillet. She refuses to let him go. She blames Catherine for everything. She's intent on *'removing the obstacle'* from her path.'"

Adrien forced his eyes to focus on the parchment in his hands, scanning its contents. Charlotte's venom astounded him, his heart quickening with each incensed, irrational word she wrote. Her final phrase knocked the breath from his lungs.

. . . and I have the means to do it.

Jésus-Christ! Terror slammed into him. Adrien snagged his baldric and ran from the room in the direction of the stables, his uncles on his heels.

*****

Pushing the horses to their limit, Adrien and his uncles raced toward Lagny, only to be halted abruptly upon entering the town.

Adrien's heart plummeted.

Shops on the main floors, homes directly above, the roads and abodes were filled with activity; the streets chaotic and clogged. Its calamity spiked his frustration and anxiety as Adrien and his uncles maneuvered their way through the mass, unable to race the final stretch of the two-and-a-half-hour journey.

Two-and-a-half torturous, fear-leaden hours.

The sun burned down upon him. Wiping the sweat from his brow with a sweep of his sleeve, Adrien desperately searched for the inn. Shouts from the windows above, haggling merchants and customers, squeals and laughter of dashing children, and the nickering of horses clashed together, and yet it was all a distant din. Adrien's heart was pounding so fiercely, it resonated in his ears, muffling the noise.

"You there!" he called out to a pauper who caught his eye in the throng. "Where is the inn?"

"To the left." He pointed up the street. "The first street to the left, my lord."

Adrien's gaze darted in the direction. It wasn't far, but with the congestion before him, it was going to take a while. He tossed the pauper a coin and began shouting to those blocking his path. It moved people along. Too slowly. It was all too damned slow!

Every horrible scenario of what Charlotte might do tormented his mind and twisted his entrails. He prayed, he prayed, he prayed he was in time.

From her note, Charlotte wasn't going to stop until Catherine was dead. Even more terrifying was the fact that Catherine was completely unaware Charlotte had been Baillet's mistress. His sister could easily fabricate an explanation as to why she was at the inn.

Catherine wouldn't have any reason to mistrust her.

Would Baillet notice Charlotte? Would he somehow foil her plans? Adrien desperately hoped so.

Finally turning the corner, Adrien spotted the inn at the end of the cobblestone road that was lined by three-story half-timbered buildings. He was almost there. His heart hammered harder. The inn was ever nearing. But not fast enough. *Merde.* Too many carts, horses, and people were in the way. Every minute mattered. Ready to jump out of his very skin, Adrien could wait no longer.

He leaped off his horse in the middle of the street, leaving it for his uncles to attend to, pushing and shoving his way through the afternoon crowds. His destination—the front doors of the inn.

The moment he tore across its threshold, he stopped dead in his tracks, giving his eyes a moment to adjust to the darker interior. He heard weeping. A woman's tears.

Scanning the few occupants in the room, some standing, some seated at the tables before him, he spotted Catherine's maid and Baillet in the far corner.

Odette pleaded. And wept.

His blood froze. Seeing how distraught she was, he knew he was too late. Dear God, something had happened to Catherine.

The maid met his gaze. "Monsieur!" She rushed to him.

Adrien gripped her shoulders. "What has happened?"

Tossing a quick glance about, Odette lowered her shaky voice, "Your sister . . . she has . . . poisoned my madame. My sweet, kind madame." Her chin dropped. She wept harder, her shoulders shaking.

Adrien's knees almost gave way.

"Y-Your sister has locked herself in one of the rooms upstairs, and won't come out," she bemoaned. "Sh-She has the antidote. She won't hand it over. I don't know if it's too late. I don't know what poison she gave her." Tears welled from her eyes. "She's in a terrible way. . . .and Monsieur de Baillet refuses to help. He—He is leaving."

Baillet approached then, his expression bland. "That's correct. I am leaving." He looked pointedly at Adrien. "I hope you enjoyed fucking my betrothed. It seems you did such a thorough job of it, she's no longer interested in marrying me. None of this"—he gestured toward Odette—"is any of my concern."

"You would actually leave her to *die?*" Adrien asked, stunned.

"As I said, this isn't my problem. I do, however, intend to speak to His Majesty about your sister. I feel it is my duty to rid society of this madwoman. She tainted the broth and then admitted to it. For God's sake, she could have killed me."

Adrien snapped. Grabbing Baillet by the lapels of his justacorps, he slammed him backward onto a nearby table.

"You are to blame for all of this!" Adrien bellowed.

Baillet stared up at him, his eyes wide with fear. "Un-Unhand me!" His hands flew to Adrien's wrists, but he couldn't pry himself loose.

"You toyed with Charlotte's affections! You used her. You misled her into thinking you cared. *You* brought this on!" He pulled Baillet up then slammed him back down, so that his head struck the table with brute force. Baillet yelped. "You'll not speak a word of this to the King, Madame de Maintenon, or anyone, for if you do, I'll call you out, and end your worthless life."

"Your—your sister poisoned a lady. That is against the law!" Baillet was foolish enough to protest.

"It will be Catherine's word against yours, since she is the one lying on a bed right now. Not you."

Adrien released Baillet.

Baillet sat up and smoothed his jacket. "If she lives."

Rage exploded inside him. Adrien smashed his fist into Baillet's jaw, knocking him off the table and onto the stone floor.

"Adrien!" Paul rushed in and grabbed his arm, Robert and Charles following directly behind. "Leave him to us. Go help your lady."

Charles and Robert were already yanking a disoriented Baillet to his feet none too gently.

Adrien turned and ran up the stairs, two at a time. Odette was quickly on his heels, calling out which room. Upon bursting into Catherine's room, the air shot out of his lungs, the sight before him hitting him like a physical blow. Leaving him cold and breathless.

Her auburn hair was fanned out on the pillow. A delicate hand clutched her stomach as she softly moaned and writhed, eyes shut. Horrified, he moved closer.

She was pale, so pale. Her complexion almost gray.

Odette sobbed anew. "The pain gets worse at times. She had the tainted broth over an hour ago . . ."

Adrien sank down on the edge of the bed, taking Catherine's hand in his. Her skin was cold. Clammy.

She opened her eyes. "Adrien," she breathed.

A knot welled in his throat. He pressed a kiss to the back of her hand "I am here, *ma belle*."

"Your sister and Baillet . . ."

"I should have told you she was his mistress," he choked out. "I'm sorry."

Again he kissed her hand again, fighting to maintain his composure. "Please forgive me, for . . . not being forthright, about my sister, about my affections. I love you." Tears blurred her sweet face. He cupped her cheeks. "I am going to make this right. Stay strong. You are going to be fine. I'll make certain of it." He kissed her brow. "I love you, Catherine."

A small smile graced her lips as a single tear slipped out of the corner of her eye.

*****

"Charlotte!" He smashed his fist against her locked door, her room close to Catherine's. "Open this door."

Silence.

He slammed his shoulder into the wooden barrier. It gave but didn't open. "Charlotte!" With fury and fear, he slammed his shoulder into the portal once more.

This time it flew open.

He found Charlotte curled up like a child, her arms tightly wrapped around her legs, crouching in the corner of the room on the floor. Her eyes red and swollen, she'd been crying extensively. She made such a pathetic sight, it momentarily unbalanced Adrien.

"*Dieu*, Charlotte, what have you done?"

Large tears streamed down her face. "I—I wanted him to . . . l-love me . . . He—He doesn't love me." She sobbed, anguished. Broken.

He crouched down to her level. "I love you, Charlotte," he said, keeping his voice soft. "I am begging you to help Catherine."

She shot to her feet, startling him. "NO!"

It was then Adrien noticed a small pouch clutched in each of her hands.

"I hate her! She has his heart." Her bottom lip quivered as she inched her way to the window. If what she had in the pouches was the antidote, he feared she'd scatter the powders to the wind.

"No, Charlotte. She doesn't. She's not going to marry him. There isn't going to be a wedding. She doesn't have his heart. He left, without a care over her condition."

Her watery eyes widened slightly. "He—He did?"

"He isn't capable of loving anyone. Please . . . Charlotte . . . Please, tell me you have the antidote."

"Of course I do. The witch advised me to purchase both . . .

in case the wrong person takes the poison. Sometimes these things are difficult to contain."

He didn't want a lengthy discussion. Or details of her misdeed. Time was of the essence. Still crouched he held out his hand. "Please, give me the antidote."

She moved closer to the window. His stomach tightened with terror.

"Why? So you can save her? You love her more than me."

He lowered his arm. "I am trying to save your life, can you not see that? If Catherine . . . dies . . . you'll be arrested and executed."

She froze.

With a strangled cry, she pressed one pouch-filled hand to her mouth. "I . . . d-don't want that." She cried hard, her shoulders slumped.

"Then give me the antidote, and I swear, I won't let anyone harm you. You'll return home. To Hôtel d'Aspe. You'll be with family who love you."

She shook her head. "No . . . noooo . . ." She moaned. ". . . I—I want to go to a cloister. The one *Maman* went to. She . . . She was h-happy there . . . I want to be happy, too."

He rose. "If a convent is what you desire, it will be so, on my word. But first, *ma chérie*"—he held out a hand again—"you must give me the antidote."

She stared at his open palm.

"*Please*, Charlotte. I love you. Let me help you. I don't want you placed in prison."

She gave him a quivering smile. "You do love me, don't you, Adrien?"

"Very much," he said from the heart.

Slowly, she stretched out her arm and held out a pouch to him.

He grabbed it from her grip. "What is in the other pouch?"

She handed him that one as well. "It is empty. It had the poison. If you want the antidote to work best, you need to mix it with wine."

Adrien shot out the door.

*****

Midnight. And still Catherine writhed.

In and out of consciousness since Adrien had given her the wine-based concoction, she looked no better. He paced. He prayed. By the predawn hours, he was beside himself, fear and worry clawing at his vitals.

What if the witch who had sold Charlotte the antidote had lied? What if the concoction he'd given Catherine was merely crushed herbs that did nothing at all?

She was still now. Far too still. Trapped in a deep slumber. One he couldn't rouse her from.

Sitting on the edge of her bed, he held her hand, the nearby candelabra illuminating her sleeping form and her lovely peaceful face in the darkened room. Dear God, he couldn't lose her. Not his beloved Catherine. He couldn't stand the heart-shattering thought. She was his. His heart belonged to her. Her heart belong to him.

They belonged together.

Tenderly, he caressed her hand, watching each breath she took, willing another and another from her.

The clock on the mantel over the hearth ticked. And ticked. And ticked.

He felt damned helpless. Utterly useless. Unable to awaken her from this wretched unnatural sleep.

He wanted to do something, *anything* to help her, but there was nothing more he could do. Except wait. It was maddening to simply sit there, fighting to hold on to hope, battling against the cold dread slowly slicing through him.

Odette came each hour to check on her mistress. She'd be back in the room soon and he hated it that he'd have to tell her that there was *still* no improvement.

Adrien squeezed Catherine's hand. "*Ma belle* . . . wake up. *Please wake up* . . . " Leaning in, he pressed a kiss to her soft lips.

He heard a soft sigh. Then he felt her lips move under his.

His heart skipped a beat.

Her fingers threaded through his hair and she kissed him back.

He sat up. "Catherine!"

The dawn broke, spilling the day's first rays into the room. She was awake and her complexion had improved. *Dieu*, she was better! And she looked so beautiful.

At the commotion, Odette raced into the room. Upon seeing her mistress awake and smiling, she let out a screech of joy and rushed forward, dropping herself down on the other side of the bed. She snatched up Catherine's hand and caressed it. "Madame, you are well!"

"A bit weak, but yes, I feel much better," Catherine said.

With a giant foolish grin on her face, Odette petted her hand and stared at her as though she were gazing upon a deity. "Worry not, madame. I'll make certain you regain your strength in no time—"

Adrien cleared his throat, snagging Odette's attention.

Odette's eyes widened. "Oh . . . I'm—I'm sorry." She rose and retreated to the far corner of the room.

Catherine gazed into Adrien's light green eyes, the love that shone there making her heart sing.

"It felt as though you were asleep for a hundred years," he said.

"It has been a hundred years since you last gave me a morning kiss." She grinned. "I like being awakened like that. Now, then, was I delirious or did I hear you say earlier that you love me?"

He grinned back. "I did indeed and I will say it again and again. I love you. I can't live without you. I don't want to. The night of the masquerade, you woke me from a slumber and brought me to life, heart, body and soul. I will awaken you with a kiss for the rest of our lives. Say you'll marry me."

She was beaming, her heart nearly bursting with joy. "Yes! Yes, I will marry you." She sat up and leaned in for a kiss. Just as their lips touched, Odette broke into a loud wail, startling both Catherine and Adrien out of the moment.

Odette blew her nose in a handkerchief she'd pulled out of her bodice, then resumed her blubbering.

"Odette, there's no need to carry on. I'm going to be fine." She smiled lovingly at Adrien. "Everything is going to be better than fine."

"Madame . . ." Odette sniffled loudly. "I—I have a confession to make. I cannot carry this on my conscience anymore."

"Oh?" Catherine said. "What confession?"

"Well . . . you see . . . that—that night . . . when you asked me to add the aphrodisiac to Monsieur's wine . . ." Odette shifted nervously from one foot to another. "Well . . . I added the powder . . . but I made a *tiny* error . . . You see, it turns out I mixed up the powders I got from the apothecary . . . I gave Monsieur le Marquis something to boost his . . . digestion rather than his libido."

Catherine and Adrien locked gazes, then burst out laughing.

Adrien pulled her tightly into his arms. "It would seem, my love, that the passion between us has been real from the beginning." He gave her a soft, tender kiss that left her wanting more.

She caressed his cheek. He was hers. All hers. Forever more. "You know, if you marry me, you run the risk of easing tensions between you and the King. Your father may not think you so reckless anymore," she gently teased.

He laughed. "I love you so very much, I'm willing to marry you—even if it pleases my father."

Then Adrien kissed her soundly. It was a kiss full of passion. So full of love.

A kiss that held the promise of happiness ever after.

GLOSSARY

Antechamber
The sitting room in a lord's or lady's private apartments (chambers).

Caleçons
Drawers/underwear.

Chambers
Another word for private apartments. A lord's or lady's chambers consisted of a bedroom, a sitting room, a bathroom, and a *cabinet* (office). Some chambers were bigger and more elaborate than others. Some *cabinets* were so large, they were used for private meetings.

Chère
Dear one. (French endearment for a woman, *cher* for a man).

Chérie
Darling or cherished one. (French endearment for a woman, *chéri* for a man).

Comte
Count.

Comtesse
Countess.

Dieu
God.

Hôtel/Château
The upper class and the wealthy bourgeois (middle class) often had a city mansion in Paris (*hôtel*) in addition to their palatial country estate(s) (*château*).

Justacorps	A fitted knee-length coat, worn over a man's vest and breeches.
Le beau	Masculine word for *the handsome one or the beautiful one* (male).
Ma belle	*My beauty.* (*French endearment* for a woman)
Merde	*Shit.*
Nom de plume	Pen name.
Pour l'amour de Dieu	*For the love of God.*
Salle	*Room*
Salle de Buffet	*Dining Room.*

THANK YOU for reading SLEEPING BEAU!

Want my next release for just **99¢**? Sign up for my **99¢ New Release Alert** newsletter at www.LilaDiPasqua.com. Each new release will be **99¢** for a SHORT time only. Get notified. Don't miss out!

FIERY TALES SERIES

Novellas
Sleeping Beau
Little Red Writing
Bewitching in Boots
The Marquis's New Clothes
The Lovely Duckling
The Princess and the Diamonds

Holiday Novella
The Duke's Match Girl

Anthologies
Awakened by a Kiss
The Princess in His Bed

Full-length novels
A Midnight Dance
Undone
Three Reckless Wishes

Lila DiPasqua is a *USA TODAY* bestselling author of historical romance with heat. She lives with her husband, three children and two rescued dogs and is a firm believer in the happily-ever-after. You can find her on Facebook, Twitter, Instagram, and Goodreads!

READ AN EXCERPT OF
LITTLE RED WRITING

Nicolas de Savignac, Comte de Lambelle, is on a mission, assigned by the Crown to uncover the secret identity of the author writing scandalous stories about powerful courtiers.

He never expected his investigation would lead to his grandmother's house, or to a ravishing woman who would stir his deepest hunger . . .

LITTLE RED WRITING

Moral of the Story of Little Red Riding Hood:

One sees here that young children,
Especially pretty girls,
Who're bred as pure as pearls,
Should question words addressed by men.
Or they may serve one day as feast
For a wolf or other beast.
I say a wolf since not all are wild
Or are indeed the same in kind.
For some are winning and have sharp minds,
Some are loud, smooth or mild.
Others appear plain kind or unriled.
They follow young ladies wherever they go,
Right into the halls of their very own homes.
Alas, for those girls who've refused the truth:
The sweetest tongue has the sharpest tooth.

Charles Perrault (1628–1703)

Chapter One

"Who is *he*?" Just as the question tumbled from Anne's mouth, the man in the light gray justacorps disappeared into the crowd. Again.

Her sister Henriette glanced over her shoulder. As usual, the Comtesse de Cottineau's Saturday Salon was filled to overflowing. Though their patroness had been called away due to a family emergency, she'd insisted that Anne and her sisters carry on with the popular weekly event in her absence. Aristos and the literati who frequented her home had been admitted and were presently milling about.

Henriette turned back. "Who?"

Who indeed.

Anne was the last person to be taken in by a handsome face, but she couldn't stop herself from trying to locate the man with the disarming gray eyes. Smoky eyes that had locked with hers for several seconds and quickened her pulse. A stunning reaction on her part. Unprecedented, actually. Twice he'd drawn her attention out of the masses straight to him by doing nothing more than directing his smoldering gaze her way. Once, even when she was engaged in a fascinating discussion about Spanish literature with the Marquis de Musis. Both times the beautiful dark-haired stranger had been at a distance in a different part of the Great Room, but she felt the heat of his regard long before she spotted him.

Maddeningly, he kept vanishing into the sea of faces.

Dragging her gaze back to Henriette, Anne noticed her sister's curious expression.

"A gentleman," Anne responded. "I've never seen him before. We should welcome him, but I seem to have lost him in the crowd." She felt foolish. Stepping into the Comtesse's shoes and acting as hostess to her elite guests was daunting. Unnerving. Her jangled nerves were likely the reason for her peculiar reaction. Statesmen, lords and ladies were in attendance along with some of the most respected scholars, writers and dramatists.

Social biases set aside while under the Comtesse's roof, they gathered together each week to debate and discuss language and literature, history and philosophy.

It was thrilling. A place of enlightenment. A great honor to be in among such distinguished company. Such brilliant minds. To be part of Madame de Cottineau's Salon—one of the city's most prestigious. Born into minor nobility, with little by way of social influence and finances, Anne and her two sisters would not have been welcome had the Comtesse not taken an interest in their humble writings and agreed to sponsor their works.

But today's Saturday Salon was different. And it wasn't simply because the Comtesse was missing. Or that Anne and her sisters, Henriette and Camille, were hostesses.

It was because of a single man. A most unsettling, mysterious gentleman.

Anne and her sisters owed much to Madame de Cottineau. Making her guests feel welcome while she was away was the least they could do for her. Yet the gentleman with the disquieting gray eyes was making the task even more challenging for Anne. She should have greeted him the moment she saw him, but the impact he'd had on her unbalanced her. She lost her nerve to approach him, when courage was never something she lacked.

Henriette's gaze swept the room. "What does he look like?"

His face appeared in her mind's eye. Anne felt her cheeks warm. Dear God, she was *blushing*. And if that wasn't embarrassing enough, she was at a complete loss for words. She was a writer, and yet she couldn't conjure a phrase to adequately describe the sheer male perfection she'd seen. Not without sounding as awestruck as she felt. Like some smitten ingénue.

"Madame de Pierpont?" The Comtesse d'Azan approached and looped arms with Henriette. "Excuse me for interrupting, but the Baron de Lenoncourt has brought up the subject of the Latin classics. Come join in the discussion. You have such an interesting take on the topic."

Henriette glanced at Anne.

"Oh, you must come, too, Mademoiselle de Vignon," Comtesse d'Azan said to Anne. "You are the only one who can keep the Baron focused on one topic at a time." Softly, she laughed.

Anne smiled at the gracious comment and was about to respond when something, or rather someone, caught her eye. Over the Comtesse's shoulder, there at the back of the room, was the mysterious man.

His eyes captured hers and held her riveted, the corner of his mouth lifting into a sensual smile. Her stomach fluttered wildly. The crowd shifted and he disappeared from her seeking sight. Anne snapped out of the spell he'd cast and tamped down her ire.

Enough was enough.

It galled her that she was behaving so foolishly. She knew better. She knew the damage an attractive man could cause a woman's mind, heart and spirit.

"Madame, I would love to join you," Anne said, grasping her skirts. "But first, there is a matter I must attend to. Please excuse me." Anne turned into the throng and made her way toward the back corner where she'd last seen the enigmatic stranger.

A smile firmly in place, she moved through the crowd, exchanging brief pleasantries along the way, behaving as any cordial hostess should. Just as soon as she located the man with the silvery eyes, she intended to extend him every courtesy. She'd welcome him to Madame de Cottineau's home. And respond to him no differently than to any other guest present.

So why were her insides still quivering?

*****

"She approaches. What do you think, Nicolas, is she the one?" Thomas, Comte de Gamory, asked near Nicolas's ear.

Nicolas de Savignac studied the woman in the blue gown as she made her way through the mass. Anne de Vignon. The middle sister. He'd overheard one of the guests point her out. Thanks to the sheer numbers in the room, he could easily hide in plain sight and observe her and her two siblings. Allowing them to see him only when he wished it.

Anne's bright red curls lightly swept her bare shoulders each time she turned her head to acknowledge one of the guests. The color of her hair was extraordinary. He was gripped by a powerful urge to run his fingers through the fiery-colored locks.

She wasn't at all what he'd expected a spinster poetess to look like. He was expecting someone rather plain. This woman was ravishing. The extent of her allure, a surprise. As was the bolt of heat that shot through his veins and tightened his groin the moment their gazes met.

He didn't like surprises.

He was still reeling over the fact that their investigation had led him to *this* hôtel, of all places. To the home of one of his very own relatives.

Discreetly, Anne glanced here and there. It was obvious to him, if no one else, that she was hunting for him. What she didn't know was that he was the one doing the hunting. That he was relentless in his pursuits, cunning enough to earn the nickname *le Loup*—the Wolf.

And he was here to catch his prey.

"*Nicolas?*"

He pulled his gaze from the redheaded beauty back to Thomas. His friend was frowning. It took some getting used to, seeing him out of his Musketeer uniform and in formal attire. Or in being out of uniform himself. But to walk in wearing the distinct blue tabard would have alerted everyone, especially the sisters in question, that he and Thomas were part of the King's private Guard. Newly promoted, Nicolas intended to prove to his King, his Captain, and the rest of the men that he deserved the honored position. That he could be as good a Musketeer, if not better, than his late legendary brother, David—Musketeer extraordinaire. Nicolas had, after all, easily beaten out other highly qualified noblemen for one of the coveted few spots. On his own. By *his* skill. *His* abilities. Just as he expected to. Once he set his mind on attaining a goal, he was unstoppable. And nothing was going to keep him from successfully completing this mission—a mission His Majesty wanted kept most quiet and accomplished posthaste.

"Well?" Thomas asked. "What do you think? Is it her or one of her other two sisters?"

Nicolas gazed once again at his object of interest. Anne had stopped and was speaking to a group of ladies.

"I don't know." *Merde.* How he wished he did. From the information he'd gathered, Anne de Vignon was the author of two volumes of poetry. He'd read them both. He'd read all the books the three sisters had written. Each woman had a distinct writing style—dark, romantic, humorous—and yet, he still wasn't certain who wielded the poisonous pen.

Now that Anne was closer, he could better appreciate the womanly details of her form. No doubt about it, both far and near, she was comely in the extreme. Her gown, though not as costly as the others in the room, accentuated her curves in the most delectable way. With the discerning eye of a libertine, he took note of her creamy skin, the slight blush to her cheeks, and the rise and fall of her breasts, her breathing a bit too quick, belying her mask of composure.

Under the unruffled façade she was discomposed. And it was because of him.

There had definitely been a mutual attraction. He'd seen it in her eyes. If used correctly, it could be a delicious advantage. He wasn't above using whatever means necessary to uncover the identity of the anonymous author who wrote under the *nom de plume*, Gilbert Leduc.

"She is beautiful," Thomas murmured. "I don't know about you, Nicolas, but I'd rather fuck a woman who looks like that, than arrest her."

"You'll not touch her." *Dieu*, that sounded absurdly possessive.

Thomas chuckled. "So you've set your sights on Anne, *le Loup*? Poor woman. She doesn't stand a chance. Curious, why her? Why not one of the other two sisters?" He gave a nod in their general direction. Both were on the opposite side of the room, engrossed in conversation. "They're comely, too."

Indeed. All three sisters had the same beautiful fiery-colored hair. Henriette de Pierpont was the eldest and the only one to marry. Widowed four years, she was attractive in her own right. As was the youngest, Mademoiselle Camille de Vignon.

But there was something about Anne . . .

"We're here to discover which sister is the author of the pen portraits and bring her before His Majesty. As ordered. Whichever will confess to the truth is the one I'm interested in," Nicolas said. Those who were patrons of the arts and had enough coin couldn't collect unsanctioned books fast enough.

Nicolas had uncovered the underground press that was printing the illegal volumes of short stories. He and Thomas had spent weeks surreptitiously watching the Parisian publisher, observing the comings and goings at his print shop, and following messenger boys until Nicolas was finally led to the home of the Comtesse de Cottineau—and the three authors who resided there.

Everyone was talking about the anonymously written stories. Everyone had a strong opinion on what should be done about the author. The women praised the writer. The men, especially those who were the subject of ridicule in the published tales, demanded justice.

Pen portraits were nothing new. Many writers used real people—mostly members of the upper class—as characters in their books. Names were changed, but the author always made it easy to identify the person being portrayed by the fictitious character. Characters that were always written with a flattering slant. However, the author of *these* pen portraits did just the opposite. This author maligned and mocked men. Important men. Powerful men. Mercilessly. It was out of control.

Anne stepped away from the women and continued on, getting nearer, her lovely dark eyes still searching for him. Unable to spot him.

His lips twitched as he held back his smile. *That's it. Come closer, pretty rabbit.*

It had taken some doing, but he'd managed to get the Comtesse de Cottineau out of her home, sending the old crone far away under false pretenses. He despised the woman. Had held nothing but contempt for her his entire life, and with her out of the hôtel, nothing stood between him and the three redheaded females.

He was focused. Ready.

The trap was set.

*****

He wasn't there. At the back corner of the room, Anne turned to face the crowd. She scanned the Great Room but couldn't locate the mysterious gentleman anywhere.

"Pardon, mademoiselle."

She jumped at the sound of the male voice behind her and spun around.

Vincent, the majordomo, gave a short bow. "Your pardon. I didn't mean to startle you." Tall, thin, his hair completely white, he always had the same expressionless look upon his face. A longtime loyal servant to the Comtesse, he'd been unnerving to Anne from the time she and her sisters moved in last spring. She could never decipher his emotions or what he was thinking.

"That's all right, Vincent."

"Mademoiselle, the Comte de Gamory and the Comte de Lambelle are here."

"Oh?"

"They have requested a private moment. They're in the Mercury drawing room. Monsieur de Lambelle has asked to see your sisters as well. Mademoiselle Camille de Vignon has already excused herself and is presently there."

Anne frowned. "Vincent, we cannot all excuse ourselves and disappear. What about the Comtesse's guests? Who are these men?"

"Nicolas de Savignac, Comte de Lambelle, is related to the Comtesse, mademoiselle."

She raised her brows. Her patroness? "He is?"

"Yes, mademoiselle. He is her grandson and wishes to speak to you."

Want more of LITTLE RED WRITING? Visit www.liladipasqua.com/the-fiery-tales/little-red-writing/